PURR-FECT POTIONS

A NINE LIVE MAGIC MYSTERY

DANIELLE GARRETT

BEECHWOOD HARBOR MAGIC MYSTERIES

Murder's a Witch

Twice the Witch

Witch Slapped

Witch Way Home

Along Came a Ghost

Lucky Witch

Betwixt: A Beechwood Harbor Collection

One Bad Witch

A Royal Witch

First Place Witch

Sassy Witch

The Witch Is Inn

Men Love Witches

Goodbye's a Witch

BEECHWOOR HARBOR GHOST MYSTERIES

The Ghost Hunter Next Door

Ghosts Gone Wild

When Good Ghosts Get the Blues

Big Ghosts Don't Cry

Diamonds are a Ghost's Best Friend

Ghosts Just Wanna Have Fun

Bad Ghosts Club

Mean Ghosts

SUGAR SHACK WITCH MYSTERIES

Sprinkles and Sea Serpents

Grimoires and Gingerbread

Mermaids and Meringue

Sugar Cookies and Sirens

Hexes and Honey Buns

Leprechauns and Lemon Bars

NINE LIVES MAGIC MYSTERIES

Witchy Whiskers

Hexed Hiss-tory

Cursed Claws

Purr-fect Potions

Furry Fortunes

Talisman Tails

Stray Spells

Mystic Meow

Catnip Charms

Yuletide Yowl

Paw-ful Premonition

Growling Grimoire

MAGIC INN MYSTERIES

Witches in the Kitchen

Fairies in the Foyer

Ghosts in the Garden

HAVEN PARANORMAL ROMANCES

Once Upon a Hallow's Eve

A TOUCH OF MAGIC MYSTERIES

Cupid in a Bottle

Newly Wed and Slightly Dead

Couture and Curses

Wedding Bells and Deadly Spells

*T*here are few things worse than an uncomfortable dinner party. Or, at least, few that I could think of as I pushed my fork through the whipped potatoes on my plate.

Seriously, why wasn't anyone *saying* anything? The silence was deafening. I managed to keep a polite smile firmly plastered on my face, even as my mind swirled with possible conversation starters. But as I jettisoned each one in rapid succession, the uncomfortable lull stretched. The only sound in the overdecorated dining room was the sterling silver utensils clanking against the gold-rimmed fine china plates.

At least the food was good. If I were indulging in the meal without an audience, I had no doubt I'd have wolfed down the entire plate already. As it was, I took careful, small bites as I carved into what I could only assume was one-hundred-dollar pot roast accompanied by a mouthwatering mushroom gravy, the whipped potatoes, and a mix of pearl onions and glazed carrots.

It was my guess that the food was catered, or maybe prepared in house by a private chef. I made a mental note to ask Clint about it later. His mother was the one hosting us, but I knew she hadn't cooked. If the formidable Ms. Cleaver, formerly Mrs. Bridges, had ever cooked, those days were long gone now. Even before her health began to fail, she'd employed a houseful of staff to see to her every need.

I glanced up from my plate and noticed Clint giving me a concerned look. We'd joked on the drive over about whether or not to come up with some sort of code word. A verbal rip cord we could pull if things got too awkward. We arrived before landing on one, and the joke fizzled as we walked up the stamped driveway to his mother's front door.

I tried to manage a restrained smile in his direction, if only to reassure him I was still hanging in there (albeit by a thread). However, I wasn't sure how convincing I looked. It wasn't his fault his mother was frosty enough she could live quite happily in her fancy Sub-Zero fridge. Our relationship was still in the early phase, where little things could all too quickly become big things. I didn't want this tension between me and his mother to cause issues.

Smiling, I reached for the stem of my wineglass and brought the burgundy liquid to my lips. I was too tense to really savor it, but the oaky flavor left a pleasant aftertaste. "This was a lovely meal, Sandra. Thank you for having us," I said, my voice coming out stiffer than I intended.

Clint's mother lifted her white linen napkin from her lap and brought it to her lips. She dabbed the fabric at the corners of her mouth with a frail and bony hand. Her coloring was paler than the last time I'd seen her.

"If you've finished, we can have a nightcap in the formal living room," she replied, her tone commanding, leaving no room for objection. Underneath the soft glow from the chandelier above our heads, her white hair took on a golden tone, making her look all the more regal and refined.

She pointed a spindly finger in the direction of the east wing of the estate and nudged her chin in that general area. "I have yet to properly entertain since the remodeling work was completed."

I bristled. A root canal sounded more tempting, but how could I protest without sounding rude about it?

The heat of Clint's expectant stare burned through me, but I didn't meet his gaze because I knew if I did, I would crack. Instead, I cast Sandra a polite smile through pinched lips and set my fork aside. "That's a very kind offer."

It wasn't a decline, but it wasn't exactly an acceptance, either.

"If you'll excuse me, I just need to visit the ladies'

room for a moment." This time I met Clint's dark, hazel eyes.

The faint lines at his eyes crinkled as he cringed. He wasn't thrilled by the idea of staying either, but we both knew we would anyway. He offered a grateful smile as I pushed back from the table.

"I'll be right back," I said, more as an assurance to Clint than anything. The large, lakeside estate had a lot of doors; it would be easy enough to slip out of one and disappear into the night.

"I'll get these dishes out of the way," Clint said as I exited the large formal dining room.

Sandra said something I didn't quite catch. Her voice was still commanding, but it was weaker, raspier, than it had been on my last visit. She was in the final stages of a terminal illness, and I knew that weighed heavily on Clint, especially as their relationship had fractured over the years leading up to her diagnosis. Sandra had the best team of healers to fuss and fret over her, making sure she was comfortable and had everything she needed twenty-four-seven, but I knew Clint wanted to make himself useful to her as well.

My heart went out to the woman's circumstances, but it was hard to make a real connection with her. She was aloof and prickly even on her best days. Every attempt I made at finding common ground was quickly batted aside by one of her barbed comments or steam-rolled by general disinterest.

With a heavy sigh, I clasped my hand around the pewter knob of the nearest powder room and pressed the door shut with my opened palm. I flicked on the lights and caught my reflection in the mirror. I wasn't sure exactly what type of woman Sandra wanted for her son, but I got the clear impression that I didn't fit the mold. If I had to guess, I'd say Sandra imagined a willowy blonde, with legs for days, bright blue eyes, a dazzling toothy smile, and nary a wrinkle or freckle.

If I stood next to Gisele Bündchen, I'd look like a hobbit.

At least my toes weren't furry.

Scoffing, I tossed my head and stared up at the ceiling. "Pull yourself together, Cora. You can do this."

Giving myself a pep talk helped bring my mood up a notch, but I needed more reinforcement. I decided to call in for backup.

Leanna answered on the second ring with a chipper, "Hey, lady!"

"*Hey*," I replied, keeping my voice quiet.

"Why are you whispering?" Leanna asked.

"I'm still at Clint's mom's house," I said as I crossed the small room. I put the lid of the toilet seat down and parked my rear on it.

"Oh, that's *right*," Leanna declared. "I forgot that was tonight. How's it going?"

I hunched over and dug my elbows into my thighs, chewing on my bottom lip. "I'm contemplating

5

whether or not I could fit through the window in the powder room."

Leanna snorted. "That bad, huh?"

"It's just a little daunting. Sandra barely said a word through the meal. She just kind of stares at me, like I'm on display in a zoo or something."

"How's Clint doing?"

"Fine. I guess." I straightened my posture and stared ahead at the vanity. "He's used to her judgment though."

I tugged at my constricting stockings that refused to yield even the slightest bit. "I can't wait to get home and jump into leggings." I readjusted the black pumps on my feet. "You have no idea how badly my heels are killing me. I'm getting blisters just *looking* at these shoes."

Leanna giggled. "Oh, come on. It's fun to get dressed up every now and then."

I released a scoffing snort from the back of my throat. "Easy for *you* to say. *You* look cute in anything. You could wear a garbage bag and make it look good."

"Honey, I'm a fashionista, not a miracle worker," Leanna retorted with a laugh.

"I don't want to go back out there."

"If you don't, they might come looking for you to make sure you didn't 'fall in.'"

I rolled my eyes. "Stop it."

"You can do this," Leanna said.

"Is that the best you can come up with?" I whispered, trying to calm my pounding heart.

"You've got nothing to worry about, babe. Clint's crazy about you. He's not the kind to get all worked up about what his mother thinks. This is just a formality. Appease the old crone and you can go home."

I stood up at the sound of footsteps in the hallway. "Right. I gotta go."

I hung up just as Leanna was saying goodbye and shoved my phone back into the pocket of my dress.

After quickly washing my hands, I cracked open the door and poked the pointy tip of one shoe over the threshold. I wasn't sure who the footsteps had belonged to, as no one was in the hall. Then again, Sandra probably preferred her staff be neither seen nor heard, unless requested.

As I moved toward the formal living room, my ear perked at the sound of muted voices. I paused to the left of a large sculpture in the foyer and drew in a steadying breath.

"Remember our deal, Clint," Sandra's raspy voice drifted.

Deal? My brow furrowed as I leaned a little closer, while keeping my cover behind the statue.

"Please don't start with that," Clint replied. He sounded tired. "Not tonight."

"Well, I assumed you forgot what we talked about," Sandra replied.

"I haven't forgotten," Clint all but growled. I'd never heard him like that before and it made my heart lurch. "Just stay off my back about it, will you?"

Sandra released a condescending laugh that made my skin crawl. "What did you expect me to say? I assumed you brought her here to gain my approval."

"You asked me who I was seeing," Clint replied. "I thought bringing her here for dinner would be a nice gesture. If I thought this was some kind of audition, I would have never suggested it."

Sandra laughed again, though it hitched midway and turned into a nasty cough.

"Here, drink some water," Clint said, his tone more patient. "Please, Mother, let's drop this conversation. I'll take Cora home and let you get some rest."

"She's not for you," Sandra said when she got her sputtering cough under control.

My blood ran cold.

"Mother…"

"I'm only stating the truth, Clint. She's not suitable."

"And why is that?" Clint's voice was glacial. I could only imagine the look in his eyes.

"Perhaps she would make a suitable mother. She's certainly got the figure to carry a pregnancy. Good birthing hips. I'll give her that. But she'll never fit into our circle."

Heat spread from my neck to my cheeks, then around my ears. I struggled to contain a tidal wave of emotion, but my tears had a mind of their own and quickly blurred my vision.

"Mother!" Clint snapped.

"What?" Sandra asked, all innocence and light.

I wanted to run. My leg muscles quivered, but I couldn't make them move. Something rooted me in place, as if my feet were encased in concrete.

A prickle on the back of my neck alerted me of someone's presence behind me. When I turned my head, my eyes met with a dark-haired woman in her midfifties. She wore teal medical scrubs and held a small pill bottle in her hands. She winced at me, and I knew she'd heard the awful things Sandra had said. Somehow that made it worse. Not only was Sandra humiliating me in front of Clint, but now a perfect stranger got to hear it, too.

The woman's eyes flitted to the archway leading to the living room, then darted back to mine. Wordlessly, she beckoned me with her empty hand. I gave the living room a pained look, then swiped at the tears splashed across my cheeks and followed the healer.

She led me into the kitchen and quickly filled a glass with water from the dispenser mounted to the sink. The kitchen was sterile and cold, like something meant to go in a restaurant. My own kitchen was cluttered with appliances, knickknacks, and usually a good smattering of dirty dishes. Sandra's kitchen stood in stark contrast, without so much as a crumb or stray loaf of bread sitting out on the miles of marble countertop.

The healer set the glass of water on the large island and gestured for me to take it. "I'm sorry you had to hear that." The woman kept her voice low and inconspicuous. Her lips were thin under the tranquil light; her cheeks looked more ashen than they had in the hallway.

"It's okay," I said as I shoved my hands into the pocket of my dress and shifted my weight with an awkward balance.

Clint would probably start to wonder where I was soon.

The healer frowned at me. "It's most definitely *not* okay."

Heat spread across my cheeks and chest. "Well, I just mean ... what can I really do about it?"

The healer's eyes scanned the room before she spoke again, and it was with a careful whisper. "Ms. Cleaver can be very cruel. You have no idea how many people I've seen come and go since I started working here six months ago."

I winced. "I can only imagine."

The nurse straightened and snatched the pill bottle back from where she'd set it on the counter before getting the glass of water. "*Anyway*, I just wanted to apologize on her behalf."

"You don't have to do that, but that's nice of you to offer." I started to turn away, but then stopped myself.

Glancing at the woman, I twisted my fingers together. "Do you—do you by chance happen to know what she was referring to when she said, 'we had a deal,' to Clint?"

The woman's eyes flashed with recognition, but her posture stiffened. "It's not really my place to say anything about that."

"So you *do* know what she was talking about?"

The woman's eyes crinkled at the edges. "Well, to tell you the truth, I did hear—"

Impatient footsteps sounded behind me and the healer scurried out of the kitchen before I could even try to wheedle the information out of her. I turned to see who had spooked her and found Clint barreling into the kitchen. He was wearing the black wool coat and held my jacket in one hand. "There you are," he said. "Come on. It's time to call it a night."

He held open my coat and I quickly stepped into it. Once bundled, he wrapped his arm around my shoulders and began shepherding me through the house to the front door.

"Is everything all right?" I asked, not sure if I should confess what I'd overheard.

"Mother needs to rest," Clint replied, his jaw tense.

We paused briefly at the archway of the living room. Sandra sat in a chair, a thick blanket draped over her legs. The healer I'd met in the hall stood to her right, fussing with an assortment of items on the table beside her.

Sandra's eyes were narrowed; a darkness flickered inside them.

"Good night, Mother," Clint said, offering a small nod.

Sandra's lips went white as she pressed them together.

"Thank you for dinner," I mumbled in a diluted voice, shivering as her frigid demeanor swept over me.

Her eyebrows formed a straight row of scrutiny as her gaze tracked my every movement.

With a wave of a veiny hand, we were dismissed. Clint started to open his mouth, only to slam it shut again. "Come on," he muttered to me.

We stepped outside in the chilly air.

Clint's hand was on the small of my back as he guided me down the porch steps. "Let's get out of here."

IT WASN'T a long drive from Clint's mother's mansion to my modest home in the heart of Winterspell. There was a strained silence between us during the ride, neither of us sure what to say. When Clint parked in my driveway, he sighed heavily and let his eyes fall closed. When he opened them again, he swiveled them in my direction. "I'm sorry tonight was so awful. I don't think she was feeling well."

I forced a smile. "It's all right."

Clint reached for the keys in the ignition. "Do you want some company?"

My gaze fell to my lap, and I shook my head. "Not tonight. I have a busy day tomorrow, so I should just get to bed."

"Right."

My heart wrenched at the disappointment in his voice, but I wanted to go inside and lick my wounds in private. I reached across the center console and squeezed his hand. "I'll see you soon."

Clint's eyes glittered under the lamplight cast down the driveway from my porch. "We're still on for bowling tomorrow night, aren't we?"

"Oh. Right. Um, I'll have to see. Like I said, tomorrow is kind of a busy day. A whole shipment of inventory came in this afternoon. It's all still in boxes. I haven't gone through *any* of it yet. So, let's play it by ear. Okay?"

"Cora, I'm really sorry about tonight." His thick brows knit together. "I wish I could erase the whole evening."

"Don't worry about it." I pulled my hand from his and reached for the passenger door.

"Are you upset with me?"

"No. Of course not." I rubbed the top of my forehead and sighed. "I'm just really tired, and Selene is probably inside, waiting to be fed, and you know how she gets."

Clint breathed a soft laugh. "Right. Well, at least let me give you a kiss good night."

I leaned toward him and closed my eyes. Our mouths met, and our lips brushed together. It wasn't a sweeping kiss filled with passion and desire. But there was still something comforting and nice about it.

I smiled as I pulled away. "Good night, Clint."

I exited the car and hurried up the front steps, already digging into my purse for my key ring. He waited until I'd opened the front door before backing out of the drive, and I stood outside a moment longer to watch him drive away.

Exhaling, I shuffled inside and barely had time to switch on the light before I felt a furry tail whipping at my ankles.

"Finally, you're home," Selene drawled as if I'd been gone for six years instead of a mere few hours.

The sleek blue-gray cat leapt onto the arm of the sofa and gave me an incredulous stare, her ethereal blue eyes glowing.

Grinning, I decided to toy with her a bit. "Awe, you missed me that much?" I reached out and tried to scratch behind her ear, but she jumped away, having none of it.

"Ha!" Selene declared, puffing out her chest. "Don't flatter yourself."

"What has you all wound up, then?" I shimmied out of my jacket and placed it on the coatrack.

"You have *no* idea what you missed while you were

gone." Selene hopped onto the back of the couch cushion and padded across, her tail sashaying with each step.

I yawned and stretched. "Enlighten me, then."

"One of the neighbor's dogs got loose again."

"Oh no." I shuffled to the fridge and opened it, searching the door for a water bottle. When I found one, I plucked it out and unscrewed the lid, guzzling down about half of it before I came back for air again.

"It was that *awful* golden retriever," Selene snarled as I stepped back into the living room.

"That cute puppy?"

The fur on Selene's back spiked. "*Cute*? I'd hardly call that *monster* cute."

I laughed. "So? What happened next?"

"He *peed* on our tree, that's what happened next," Selene shouted as if the dog had committed murder in front of her.

"Wow," I deadpanned. "That's terrible."

Selene's whiskers twitched. "Don't patronize me."

I plopped down on the couch and stretched my legs out across the coffee table in front of me. "I'm not."

"*Anyway*, I took care of the matter myself, thank you very much."

I leaned forward. "What did you do?"

"Taught the little devil a lesson, that's what."

"Selene…"

"Alright, fine. I burst out the kitty door and used a zest of magic on its rear end while it was in the middle of doing its business. The mangy thing scrammed after that."

"What have I said about using your magic when I'm not here?" I made a clicking noise with my tongue.

"He deserved it, if you ask me," Selene declared.

"Well, thanks for keeping the yard safe," I said.

"Someone has to," Selene responded, oblivious to my sarcasm.

When she turned to me, some of the confidence in her gait waned and she slumped, parking her furry rear on the cushion closest to me.

"So, how's lover boy?" the cat asked, her eyes shifting to the large window behind me for a moment. "Normally you two come in here all hot and heavy."

"Let's just say it was a bit of a rough night."

"What happened?"

I gazed up at my familiar and tried to smile, but it was meager at best. "Turns out Clint's mother is not my biggest fan."

I proceeded to give her the scoop. When I finished the story, winded and spent, Selene sat up straight, her ears alert like a Doberman. "I say we go back over there and hex the miserable old biddy in her sleep!" she exclaimed.

I chuckled and crossed one ankle over the other. "As tempting as your offer sounds, I think I'm going to have to pass on that one."

"Why?" Selene wrinkled her nose in disappointment.

"Mainly, because I've heard the beds in prison don't come with memory foam toppers," I teased.

"Bah. That only matters if we get caught!" Selene protested.

"Right." I laughed softly and reached for the remote control.

"Fine, fine. Well, in that case, there's only one solution," Selene replied. "Trash TV and a bowl of extra-buttery popcorn."

Smiling, I clicked on the TV. "How do you know me so well?"

"No offense, Cora, but you're a little predictable."

I smiled and reached toward her. This time she let me scratch behind her ear and I even got a little purr out of her.

A commercial blared and I summoned the energy to get off the couch. "I've gotta get out of these nylons before they cut off any more blood flow."

"Then you'll make the popcorn?" Selene asked.

"Yeah."

"Don't forget the extra butter!"

"I won't. After all, I've got to keep my 'baby-making hips' in good working order," I groaned.

"Uh, Cora?"

"Hmm?"

"I think you mean '*birthing* hips,'" she corrected. Her tail twitched. "The baby-making part comes before that."

"Oh *geez*, Selene," I muttered, my cheeks growing

warm. "Let's not go there. Anyway, you knew what I meant."

Selene snickered as I made my way down the hall to my bedroom. "You know, I'd say either way Clint doesn't seem to be complaining!"

There went my cheeks, burning as hot as fire for the third time tonight.

2

*S*elene and I headed to Wicked Wicks early the next morning. What I'd told Clint the night before was true: it was set to be a busy day at my magical candle shop. As eager as I was to get started, my employee, Lily, appeared to be even more so, as she was already there and had the shop open fifteen minutes ahead of schedule.

"Good morning!" she greeted as Selene and I came inside.

"Morning, Lily. You're here early."

"I keep telling her she should switch to decaf," Selene muttered.

The cat wasn't much of a morning person. Er, morning feline.

Lily flashed a cheery smile as she tucked a strand of long blonde hair behind her ear. "Well, I woke up with a great idea for the display we were talking about. For the new Tahitian vanilla line."

"Oh?"

Lily had only been working for me the past few weeks, but she'd picked everything up so quickly that it was hard to remember what life was like without her in the shop. She was always in a good mood and delighted the customers. Her bubbly personality was even enough to blunt Selene's sarcastic commentary, which was saying something.

"Yeah. Here," Lily said, coming around the counter, "let me show you what I've put together so far."

I arched a brow at Selene, then followed after the young woman. Selene opted to stay behind, taking her usual perch in the cubbies behind the register where I kept custom orders awaiting pickup.

Lily took me to the endcap display and explained her ideas. I offered a few tweaks to her plan, then left her to finish it. I pointed a thumb over my shoulder. "I'm going to head to the back to start unpacking everything that came in yesterday. Try not to get too jealous of me back there having the time of my life."

Lily laughed. "I'm *totally* jealous."

"Want to trade places?" I arched a hopeful eyebrow and grinned. "It's not too late."

"Then who will mind the register?" Lily touched her finger to her chin and tilted her head to the side.

"What about you, Selene? Want to help?"

"Then who will keep Lily and the customers happy?"

I snorted. "Yeah, that's definitely what you're doing out here."

"I know how to make sales, too," the cat replied with a flick of her tail. "Just last week I talked some young punk into upping his order from three to a full half dozen candles for his mother's birthday gift. Remember that?"

"Um, I do. That was only after you nearly made him cry, guilt-tripping him over not spending enough time with his grandmother before she passed away."

Selene tilted her head to one side. "Well, every salesperson has a different bag of tricks. Personally, I find guilt to be rather effective."

Rolling my eyes, I turned around and went into the storeroom. There was no point in arguing with the prickly cat. She was ancient and beyond set in her ways.

In any case, sales were on the rise, and I was elated that business was picking up again. Within a few more weeks things should fully return to normal for the first time since I'd made my plea at the town hall meeting. Winterspell wasn't a rough-and-tumble kind of town, but there was always some kind of scandal or juicy morsel of gossip churning among the residents. I was just glad people had stopped whispering about me and my business.

I rolled up my sleeves and got to work, and a couple

uneventful hours passed by. I did my best to focus on the tasks at hand, but my mind kept obnoxiously back-tracking to the weird conversation I'd overheard between Clint and his mother last night.

What deal did they have, and what did it have to do with me?

Clint hadn't offered up any details on the ride home. I wasn't sure he knew I'd even overheard the conversation. I'd debated asking him about it, but the whole thing was so awkward.

I didn't like that he was hiding something from me, and I knew it would eventually turn to resentment. Our relationship was new and still felt fragile and uncertain in a lot of ways. Clint had moved into a rental house in town, and seemed content to stay, but I still had questions about where our relationship was headed long term.

I took a deep breath, grabbed my coat, and wandered out to the front of the shop. Selene and Lily were both at the counter, the cat sitting in judgment as Lily gift wrapped an order.

"Do you mind if I take my lunch break a little early? I need to clear my head and get some fresh air. When I get back, you can go take yours."

Lily's warm smile lit up the room. "Of course. Have at it."

Selene jumped down from her perch and sauntered my way. "I'm coming, too. A bowl of tuna is calling my name."

"When *isn't* it calling your name?" I teased.

I held the door open as Selene pranced outside, her tail swooshing proudly through the air.

"Wanna go to Whimzee's Deli?" I suggested, glancing down at Selene who strutted at my ankles.

Selene flashed her teeth, forming something of a smile. "Is that even a real question?"

I chuckled to myself. They had her favorite tuna.

We walked to the delicatessen, placed our order at the counter, then sat in a booth by the front window. Our order didn't take long as we'd arrived well ahead of the lunch rush.

Selene wasted no time chowing down on her meal.

"Easy there." I gave her a joking smile. "You're practically inhaling it, and I don't know kitty CPR."

"I'm hungry," Selene declared through a mouthful. Bits of tuna flecks were in her whiskers, and she licked them off with her long, pink tongue.

"I can tell."

I took a small bite of my salad. Selene noticed. "Is that all you ordered?" she asked.

"Selene, you were standing right next to me at the register."

The cat narrowed her eyes. "Is this because of the whole *birthing hips* debacle?"

I frowned. "Don't start."

"Come on, Cora! You can't let the old hag get into your head."

I quirked a brow. "Oh? As if you haven't made a

comment here and there about my eating habits, or, what was it you called them, *love pounds?*"

The cat swished her tail. "You know I don't mean it. I just like to try and get your goat."

Ignoring her, I plucked my phone from my purse and propped my elbows up on the table, taking a moment to scroll through my emails.

"Hmm…" I narrowed my eyes in concentration, noticing an unopened and recently received email that I hadn't been expecting.

"What is it?" Selene stopped munching and swallowed down a hefty bite before planting her eyes on me.

"I have an email from Tabitha Hardwick."

Selene's eyes widened. "Well? What does it say?"

"Hold on," I grumbled.

The email thread came up bigger on the screen. I skimmed the words quickly, while Selene's tail twitched like a metronome.

Both my brows lifted when I reached the end. "She said the private contract gig she had fell through." I paused to glance up at Selene who listened with perked ears. "She wants to know if I still need help looking for Aunt Lavender."

"What?" Selene nearly shouted. "Are you serious?"

I skimmed the short message again, making sure I wasn't misreading it. When I finished the second pass, I nodded. "Can you believe it?"

"What are you waiting for? Start tappity-tapping!"

Selene prompted, all but throwing herself across the table.

I jolted into action, quickly typing out a reply.

"Tell her we will be involved in the search. Everything goes through us first," Selene said.

I arched an eyebrow. "Won't that be insulting? I mean it's her job—"

"Tell her we demand full transparency," Selene added.

I frowned. "I think there's a more diplomatic way to—"

"Tell her you expect to see a contract and receive itemized billing for her hours. We won't play any kind of games."

"Will you stop interrupting me?" I groaned, my thumbs traveling a mile a minute as I resorted to just typing out the text myself.

"Fine." Selene rolled her eyes as if I'd just given her the worst insult ever. *"Don't* get my help. Just bear in mind *you* asked for it in the first place."

I glanced at her over the top of the phone screen. "Just finish your tuna. You're easier to get along with when your mouth is full, and you can't talk as much."

"Just because things haven't been going your way lately doesn't mean you have to take it out on me," Selene huffed.

"I just hit send."

"Good luck," Selene droned. "Not that it's any of my business."

"Oh, just stop being sullen."

I blew out a relieved breath and leaned my back against the red cushions of the booth. "Finally, a lucky break."

My appetite perked up a little and by the time I'd polished off the last bite of my salad, my phone dinged and a new message for Tabitha popped up.

"Wow. That was quick. It's Tabitha again."

I quickly read the message to myself. It was short but it was everything I had hoped to hear. I couldn't suppress an enthusiastic grin.

"Let's hear it then," Selene said, feigning disinterest with a dramatic sigh.

"She said she'll be in Winterspell tomorrow!"

3

The bell tinkled into the quiet of my candle shop. In stepped Clint, wearing black sneakers, dark denim boot-cut jeans, a navy button-down and a black, unzipped jacket.

He had a five o'clock shadow and looked a little rougher somehow. Then again, maybe that was just due to his casual attire. I was used to seeing him in a suit and tie. "Hey," he said, slipping one hand into his pocket while waving at me with the other. "I was passing by on my way back from running some errands. Thought I'd stop in and see you."

He flashed that charming smile that made my heart melt.

There were a few customers browsing the shop, but Lily had it well in hand. I pushed aside the basket of Midnight Glow candles and placed my palms on the counter at his approach. "It's a pretty nice day out there. Chilly, but sunny."

Clint smiled. "Yeah. Not too bad."

"How are you?" I asked.

"Better now that I'm here with you."

"Oh, may the goddess save me," Selene groaned from her perch over my left shoulder.

Twisting around to glare up at her, I flashed a saccharine smile. "Hairball?"

Selene ignored me and stood up, turning around to show me her rear. I got the message loud and clear.

"Sorry about her," I said, shifting my attention back to Clint.

He chuckled. "It's nice to see you, too, Selene."

The cat scoffed.

"Anyway, I came to keep you company while you close up shop for the night," he continued. "Need me to wash the windows or take out the trash? I'm at your disposal."

"You don't have to do any of that," I told him.

"I know," he said. "I want to."

"Cora, when a man offers to clean for you, you don't shoo him away," Selene muttered. "I swear. What are they teaching you young people in schools these days?"

"Come on," I said, tugging on Clint's hand.

He followed me into the storeroom, and I switched on the light. When I spotted the broom balanced in the corner, I plucked it out and handed it to him. "Knock yourself out." I grinned.

"Where do you want me to start?" Clint's eyes twinkled with more enthusiasm than I'd expected.

I tucked a strand of loose hair behind my ear and planted my hands on my hips as I pondered. "Um … you could sweep the sales floor if you want. Lily was making gift baskets earlier, so there's bits of ribbon and glitter and cellophane everywhere."

"You've got it." Clint's smile reached his eyes.

"Thank you."

He moved closer to me, tilted his head down, and gave me a deep kiss.

"I've been thinking about doing that all day," he explained when we separated a few moments later.

"*Blech.* Can you two cut it out or take it somewhere else?" Selene called from around the corner. "We can hear you two sucking face all the way out here."

"She's in a mood," Clint said with a chuckle.

"Believe it or not, she's actually being pleasant today."

"Heard that too!"

Clint led the way out of the storeroom and began sweeping. After a few passes with the broom, he began whistling.

Selene narrowed her eyes in his direction. "You're awfully bubbly this evening. All things considered."

Clint stopped sweeping and frowned up at the cat.

"What does that mean? Do I have some kind of bad omen on me or something?"

"Yeah. She's five six, wafer thin, and likes to tell you what to do with your every waking moment," the cat replied.

"Selene…" I cringed.

"Cora?" Clint swiveled his gaze to me.

I gulped and tried to busy myself with candle placement, but Clint wasn't buying it. "Okay," he said, cupping his hand over the top of the broomstick as he leaned on it for support. "Exactly *how* much did you overhear last night?"

My shoulders drooped a notch. "It's really none of my business. I shouldn't have been eavesdropping in the first place."

Clint's eyes were sympathetic, but his brows knitted with worry. "Cora, please, just tell me the truth."

My cheeks warmed as I tucked my chin down, staring at the floor. "I heard your mother say something about a deal. Then she also made a couple of unfavorable comments about my body type and pedigree."

Clint inhaled a slow, dragging breath. When he released it, he stretched his arm out, the broomstick leaning with his movement. "I'm so sorry, Cora. I wish I could say my mother is just losing it, but truth be told, she's never been the type with a filter."

He abandoned the broom and came over to me. Gently, he took me in his arms and pulled me close.

"You are perfect, and I appreciate every bit of your body."

"All right, take it easy, Romeo. There's children over there," Selene interjected.

Clint smiled. "Please, don't listen to anything she said."

"What about the deal? What was she talking about?"

Clint's face paled and his gaze flitted past my shoulder.

"Clint?" I prompted.

"Suddenly the heartthrob has amnesia?" Selene quipped.

I shushed her.

Clint winced. "It was after everything happened with the will. My mother changed it around again."

"After your brother…" I trailed off, not wanting to make the situation even more touchy by steering it in the direction of his deceased sibling.

Clint nodded, his eyes traveling downward to stare at his shoes. "Right." When he lifted his gaze back to mine, he bobbed his head. "She's leaving everything to me."

"She is?"

"Wowzers!" Selene declared. "Safe to say dinner is on you tonight, Mr. Dreamboat. I'm thinking lobster!"

Clint ignored the cat's crooning. "But there are conditions." Guilt etched across the lines in Clint's face.

"What are they?"

"Does it really matter?" Clint's hands moved lower

on my back as he drew me ever nearer. "She's not the one in this relationship."

I was torn over how to answer. It wasn't really any of my business, but I also couldn't shake that somehow one of the conditions involved me, otherwise the entire conversation I'd overheard made no sense.

"Clint, please, just tell me what's going on."

Clint stepped back and cleared his throat. "After everything that happened with Seth, she got spooked. She's worried I won't carry on our family name, our family traditions. I don't know why it's all so important to her, but she's fixated on it right now. The whole thing is tangled up with grief over losing Seth … and Melissa. She knows their relationship and future child were all a lie, but she's still grieving it all the same. As if she lost a real grandchild, rather than a figment of one."

Clint paused and rubbed at the back of his neck. I quickly glanced around, wondering if any of the customers were overhearing our Shakespearean-level drama. Lily was speaking with two ladies in the far corner of the shop, and the third customer was looking ready to exit empty-handed.

"The house will be turned over to me upon my mother's death," Clint continued, drawing my attention back to him. "However, the rest of the estate will be placed in a trust, only to be released once I reach my fifth wedding anniversary or have my first child."

I blinked at him. This certainly wasn't news I'd been expecting.

"If I don't meet those conditions, her estate and fortune will go to a charitable foundation."

I tried to brush it off as much as I could, although I was feeling more surprised than I allowed myself to let on. "So, then why not just let it all go to the charity? You've told me since the beginning that you have your own money and don't care about the inheritance."

Clint's lips pressed together, and his eyebrows formed a straight line. His cheeks flushed slightly as his gaze skated toward the window. "Well, I mean … I *did* say that. It's not like I'm going to be homeless or something tomorrow without it but…"

My heart sank. Here I thought we'd been building something on a solid foundation, only to find out it was made of sand.

"What are you saying, Clint? Do you need the money or not?"

"I promise you that the deal my mother forced me to make shouldn't change anything between us. Nor should you feel pressured in any way."

I wanted to take his words to heart, but it was easier said than done. "Well, if you don't need the money, then there's no pressure involved. Right?"

Clint raised his palms as if to wave a white flag of defeat. His head shook back and forth. "Listen, I don't want you to feel like you're being put in the middle of this weird thing I have going on with my mother."

That was one way to put it.

The lines at the side of his mouth deepened. "However, if I don't find a way out of this and my mother doesn't agree to be flexible with the inheritance, I might be forced to return to Chicago."

"Chicago?" I could barely hear the sound of my own voice over the alarm bells ringing inside my head.

Clint's nod was slow. "I will have to resume my career there. Right now, I'm only *maintaining* my income. I'm getting by, but I'm burning through my savings a lot faster than I expected to. I thought I could network and continue to build on my own, but it turns out that the in-person meetings and the wining and dining of potential clients is more of a factor than I originally thought."

I took a step backward, frowning at the floor, wishing that Clint and I were having this conversation in private and not in front of my sassy cat. However, it wasn't like I would be able to *hide* it from her either. Maybe it was best to rip off the Band-Aid and get it all out in the open from the start.

"Cora..." Clint's voice is soothing, but wasn't enough to drown out the monumental shock wave rippling through my veins.

I shook my head and blinked up at him. "I—"

"If you need some space, I'll totally understand." His jaw slackened and his eyes were as torn and tormented as I felt.

"Maybe." My voice was a shallow croak.

Clint gave me a sincere smile of apology. "I'm sorry it had to come out this way. I should have been more honest about things. I just kind of kept hoping things would turn around. I'd take one or two steps forward, just to get sent back again. And I guess I'm not used to that feeling."

"Yeah." I couldn't look at him.

"I'm gonna go," he whispered, already tracking toward the door. "If you need me, or want to talk, just give me a call."

"I will." I bobbed my head.

My ears burned. Did we just break up? Worse, in front of Selene?

I wanted to melt into the floorboards and disappear forever, but I had a business to run, and it was closing time. I grabbed the broom and picked up where Clint left off, all the while feeling Selene's eyes boring into my back.

To my surprise, she waited until we were alone, after all of the customers left, and Lily clocked out. "Are you going to wallow all night?" she asked as I locked up the register and shut off the light switches to the back of the store.

I tightened my jaw and didn't answer.

She made a purring sound as she stretched. "All right, I see how it is. The silent treatment."

"I just don't want to talk about it right now," I said, yanking my purse from the bottom shelf behind the counter.

Selene hopped onto the counter, her eyes bright. "I know what will cheer you up."

"What's that?" I asked, only half paying attention.

"A nice, *big* fish dinner."

"No thanks." The last thing I wanted to do was eat. My stomach was twisted into knots that even the most seasoned Eagle Scout wouldn't be able to untie.

"Oh, come on, it will be fun," Selene purred.

"I just want to go home and go to bed."

"Fine," Selene muttered under her breath and stalked off down to the other edge of the counter.

"You'll still get dinner, don't worry," I appeased.

"Tuna steaks?" The optimistic ring returned to Selene's voice as she tossed me a hopeful glance over her furry shoulder.

"I'll defrost them when we get home."

"Hooray!" Selene proclaimed.

At least one of us was happy.

I told myself that Tabitha was coming into town tomorrow, and that would distract me from my woes with Clint. I had more important things to worry about, but I knew it wouldn't be Aunt Lavender who haunted my dreams tonight.

*T*abitha and I exchanged a series of correspondences over the course of the evening, which culminated in plans to meet for coffee at Dragon's Gold the following day at lunch. Lily agreed to extend her shift a few hours to hold things down at the shop while Selene and I were out. It was yet another reminder of how much better my quality of life was since hiring full-time help.

Selene took the lead as we walked down the sidewalk toward the popular coffeehouse. Her tail was aloft, almost stiff, and she kept her barbed commentary to herself. When we passed a woman walking a slobbering hound dog and Selene didn't offer up a complaint about the canine's breath, I officially knew she was stressed out.

"It's going to be okay," I reminded her as I held open the door to the coffee shop.

"Of course it is. Who said anything to the contrary?" Selene asked, before sauntering inside.

Smiling, I followed and glanced around the busy dining room. Tabitha was easy to spot. I'd seen enough photos of her from her books and podcast promotional materials, and her silver-mauve ponytail stood out among the relatively subdued style choices of the other patrons. She wore a fitted leather jacket over a scoop-neck white tee and had one hand wrapped around a Dragon's Gold takeaway cup.

Selene spotted her too and made a quick beeline toward the table where she was sitting. A few nearby customers did a double take at the sight of a cat prancing through the room, but no one complained to me as I followed behind her.

"Hello, Tabitha?"

Tabitha raised her gaze, her red lipstick a sharp yet flattering contrast to her ivory skin. Her smoky eye shadow and the cat-eye tip of her eyeliner accentuated the boldness of her aquamarine eyes. Her nails were painted a lilac color, proving to be the most subtle thing about her.

Her eyes warmed as they met mine. "Hi, Cora." She gestured with her perfectly manicured nails at the empty chairs across from her. "Thank you for meeting me here."

Selene jumped into the nearest chair, leaving me to go around and take the one closest to the window.

"Thank *you* for agreeing to meet me on such short notice," I said as I settled in my chair.

"What's this *me* business?" Selene interrupted, placing her front paws on the table so she could see more easily.

Tabitha gasped softly.

"This is Selene," I explained.

Tabitha recovered from the shock quickly. "You mentioned your familiar in our correspondence, but I'll admit, I didn't expect a *talking* familiar. I'm not sure I've met one before."

Selene flashed her dainty canines. "That's because I am one of a kind."

Tabitha's eyes gleamed. "A rare treasure indeed."

Selene's ears flattened. "Don't get any ideas about putting me in a museum."

"I'm pretty sure any museum that agreed to take you would be looking to pawn you off on someone else within twelve hours," I said.

Tabitha barked a laugh. "You've got nothing to worry about, Selene."

"I can't believe you're really here," I told Tabitha. "I hope we aren't keeping you from anything."

Tabitha gave a casual flick of her wrist. "My schedule has significantly freed up, so it's no problem at all."

Tabitha and I were roughly the same age, but our life paths couldn't be more different. I'd spent my entire life in the same small town, whereas she'd traveled to some of the most remote corners of the world, seeking adventure and treasure.

"Did you want to order anything before we dive in?" Tabitha asked. A mug of steaming coffee sat on the table in front of her, along with a blueberry scone on a small white plate.

"Oh, um, I guess I should." I twisted in my seat to check out the line at the register. There were a few people waiting to order, but it wouldn't take too long.

"I'll take a saucer of oat milk," Selene interjected. "Not too hot. No foam."

Even when we were with a virtual stranger, she couldn't help herself. With a sigh, I scooted to the edge of the bench seat and got up from the table. "Yes, your highness."

Tabitha stifled a giggle as I departed.

I quickly ordered my usual drink along with Selene's milk. The barista gave me a knowing smile as I explained who it was for. The cookies in the display case called out to me, but I resisted adding one to the order. I tended to inhale my cookies, and I didn't want Tabitha to think she'd partnered up with the Cookie Monster.

When I returned to the table, Tabitha and Selene were discussing the Bermuda Triangle of all things. Tabitha shifted gears once I was seated again. "Shall we dive in?" she asked before wrapping her hands around the mug of coffee. She drew it to her lips and took a small sip before placing it on the table.

"Yes, please. Um, how do these sorts of things usually work?" I asked.

Tabitha dug into the leather satchel hanging on the back of the chair beside hers and pulled out a weathered notebook. She flipped it open to a section marked by a red ribbon and dragged one nail over the page until she found what she was searching for. "You mentioned that you found Obin's Odyssey, but that somewhere along the way the pages referring to the Golden Lotus were removed."

She glanced up from her reading and I nodded.

"Right." Her lashes fluttered downward, and she drummed her fingers on the surface of the table.

Somewhat reluctantly, I'd told her about the tome via email, but Selene and I had agreed to keep our latest discovery to ourselves. No one could know that Aunt Lavender had one half of the mysterious artifact.

"I think this is the first avenue we should explore," Tabitha said after a moment.

"You mean the missing pages?"

Her eyes drifted up to mine. "It's best if we start by trying to figure out *when* they went missing and *who* might have taken them," she explained.

"And why," Selene said, adding her two cents.

Tabitha's eyes switched to the cat, and she gave an approving nod. "Exactly."

"So, you think our hypothesis is right? Whoever took Aunt Lavender was after Obin's tome?" I asked, a gnawing sensation rolling through my stomach.

In truth, I knew it was one step closer than that. Somehow, someone had found out that Aunt Lavender had one part of the Golden Lotus. But Selene and I agreed that it was best to keep that detail to ourselves. We'd cop to her having Obin's tome. That was close enough.

Either way, it was the best theory we had for the reason behind Aunt Lavender's abduction. We'd spent weeks searching for answers, though it felt much longer. Through it all, the Golden Lotus was the only thread that connected all the dots. My gut told me we were on the right track. Though sometimes when I lay in bed tangled up between reality and dreams, I wondered if it wasn't my intuition I was feeling, but merely a coping mechanism I'd created to hold onto my last shred of hope.

Tabitha canted her head to one side as she reviewed her notes. "If your hunch is right—and for what it's worth, I think it is—then the person who abducted your Aunt Lavender is also on the hunt for the Golden Lotus. It's probably a good assumption that that same person either *has* the missing pages or is out there looking for who has the missing pages."

"She swiped the book from Salvatore Greco." I cringed a little as I gave her the answer.

If Tabitha thought Aunt Lavender's act was scandalous, she hid it well, only offering a slight nod of encouragement as I continued speaking.

"No one seems to know where Sal got the book, and

now he is dead, so we likely won't be able to find out." I sighed and pressed my shoulders against the back of the chair. I hadn't even touched my latte. My fingers trembled slightly as I grabbed the paper cup.

"Personally, I think the old coot took the pages for himself," Selene interjected.

"To what end?" Tabitha asked.

"With Sal, it always came back to money," the cat answered. She had no qualms about speaking ill of the dead, something I'd learned rather quickly. "Maybe he had a private buyer."

"Then why not sell the entire tome?" Tabitha asked.

"Again, *money*." Selene flicked her tail. "He could sell the complete tome; even with the missing section it would fetch a pretty penny. Then, he sits on the so-called *missing* pages for another handful of years, allowing time for intrigue and mystique to build to a fever pitch, and then *bam*! He comes out with another lucky discovery to cash in again."

Tabitha pursed her lips. "You're quite cynical, aren't you?"

"Lady, you don't make it through a few hundred years of life on this space rock with your rose-colored glasses intact. Survival requires cynicism. Loads of it."

I scoffed. "Well, you really might live forever, then."

Tabitha quirked one silver-hued brow. "You're immortal? How interesting!"

Selene puffed her chest. I knew what was coming

next. I could recite her whole speech even without the aid of cue cards.

"Have you heard that cats have nine lives?"

Tabitha nodded.

"And are you familiar with The Fates?"

Tabitha's eyes shifted toward me. "As in … the Greek myth?"

"Oh, I assure you, they're real," Selene said, drawing Tabitha's attention back to her. "Each life has a thread, correct? Well, in my case, being a cat and all, I had nine. By the time I got to my eighth one, I knew I wasn't long for this world. Decided I needed to take matters into my own paws if I wanted to buy myself an extended warranty, so to speak."

I planted my face in the palm of one hand.

"I cooked up a plan to take the thread of life from The Fates. No thread, no snip-snip, no dirt nap."

Tabitha laughed. "I see. And it worked? This plan?"

"No. I died." Selene flicked her tail again. "I got mowed down by a taxicab outside a froyo shop in Athens."

I blinked. I'd never heard *that* part before. "Are you serious?"

Selene glowered at me. "Of course I am. I told you this wasn't some silly story I like to trot out at parties."

"But you—I mean, they're not—"

"Real?" Selene snapped. "I can assure you they are."

"What happened next?" Tabitha prompted.

"Well, luckily for me, I'd started this journey while

on my eighth life. I revived into my latest and greatest form—" She paused to let us admire her sleek feline figure, "—and I found the old hags and got my thread! They weren't too happy about it, of course, but I got away and now the only person in the world who knows where that thread is, is me."

"Very impressive. You have to come on my podcast sometime!" Tabitha exclaimed.

I raised a finger. "I have a question."

"Oh, now she wants to talk about it," Selene quipped. "Yes, Cora?"

"Where was your guardian witch while all of this was happening? She was really okay with you gallivanting all over Greece, looking for The Fates?"

Selene's tail slumped. "Things were different then."

"How so?"

"I'm not one hundred percent sure, but I think my dependence on my guardian is either some kind of payback curse, a punishment for stealing the thread, or maybe it's always the way it goes for a feline familiar on their ninth life. A sort of baked-in protection, I suppose, stifling though it may be."

Tabitha shook her head. "I'm missing something."

"In a nutshell, Selene can't get too far away from her guardian without her magic, and eventually her life force, draining," I explained. "Technically speaking, she wasn't supposed to come to me until after Aunt Lavender passed away. But when Lavender went missing … Selene thought she'd been left behind, and she didn't want to risk withering away, so she came to me and we became bonded."

"I'm not sure I understand," Tabitha said, her eyes narrowed. "If you can't die, then what is there to fear?"

Selene's eyes closed and her whole body shuddered. "I've died eight times, in a variety of ways, but there is nothing—*nothing*—that compares to that feeling. The feeling of being abandoned. Without magic. Without purpose."

Her eyes opened slowly. "I never want to feel that way again."

Tabitha looked regretful of her question. "I see."

I ran my hand down Selene's back, smoothing the fur that remained on end. "It's worked out for the best, really. Without Selene, we might not have realized something was wrong. Aunt Lavender has always had a wanderer side. It would have taken us weeks, probably months, before we started to look for her, and by then—"

My words trailed off, too awful to voice.

"We're going to get you some answers," Tabitha said, her tone gentle, even as her eyes and jawline were set with fierce determination. "Lavender couldn't be the only one who knew that Salvatore had Obin's tome. She might not be the first—or last—victim. Whoever took her might be out on the prowl."

"While we look for Aunt Lavender, we might be able to save someone else in the process," I suggested.

Tabitha smiled, her face bright and eager. "Kill two birds with one stone."

"Multitasking at its finest."

"Teamwork makes the dream work." Tabitha's laughter tinkled like a wind chime.

I wanted to ensconce myself in her optimism but couldn't fully banish the dark clouds swirling around my shoulders.

5

"*E*verything is all good here," Lily declared.

"Are you sure?" I stood on the concrete steps leading up to the library while Tabitha and Selene waited for me by the doors. I pushed a finger against my ear to hear Lily better over the whoosh of a passing truck.

"I'm *positive*," Lily said, her voice smooth and confident.

"Has it been busy since we left?" I asked.

"Steady," Lily said, "but not overwhelmingly so."

I took a deep breath and glanced at Tabitha and Selene. "All right. Thanks. If I need you to close up later, can you do that?"

"Not a problem," Lily chuckled. "I can handle it."

"You're the best," I said. "Thank you so much."

"You know I'm here for you when you need it," Lily declared.

The authenticity in her voice made my heart swell. I vowed to give her a raise whenever I was in a place to afford it.

I hung up and stepped inside the multistory library with Tabitha and Selene. We found a cozy spot in the back corner of the second floor, where we knew that we wouldn't be bothered and would have a decent amount of privacy to sit and talk, uninterrupted.

Tabitha stretched her long legs out in front of her as she got comfortable in a large, eggshell-white chair. We got her up to speed on what we had worked on thus far, regarding our own research and investigation into Lavender's disappearance. Tabitha took some notes, nodding along in acknowledgement every so often, and gave us the respect of listening intently.

As we spoke, a question loomed large in the back of my mind. There hadn't been any talk of payment in any of my correspondence with the famous witch, but now that she was here, and so willing to drop everything to help, I wondered if there was some unspoken fee being applied to the conversation. Finally, as Selene wrapped up the presentation of our findings, I broached the question. "Um, I hate to ask, but could you give me a ballpark figure for your services? Now that you know where we're at with everything." I kept my hands folded in my lap to keep from twitching.

Tabitha glanced up from her notes, her brows peaked. "You don't owe me anything, Cora. It's my privilege to help."

Relief coursed through me, though my worry was quickly replaced with a small sense of guilt. "That is very kind. Thank you." I nodded. "It seems the least we could do is invite you to join us for dinner. It's Tuesday, so we're going to my mom's place. She's a great cook, and always makes enough for twelve. If you're interested?" I glanced at Selene, then back to Tabitha. "Of course, we also completely understand if you just want to relax and spend the evening alone."

Tabitha's eyes warmed. "I'd *love* to join you for your family dinner tonight. Thank you so much for the offer."

She placed her hand to her heart, closed her notebook, and stood up.

It was the beginning of what I hoped would be a blossoming and wonderful friendship.

"Cora? Is that you, dear?" Mom called from the kitchen as I ushered Tabitha inside.

"It's me," I called back, shrugging out of my coat. "Where's Evan? I didn't see his car."

"Oh, he's on the way," Mom replied, coming out to greet me. She wore her favorite apron that had the words "Will Cook for Wine" printed on the chest.

I stepped to the side, revealing Tabitha who stood

behind me, waiting politely to be introduced to the family. "Mom, this is Tabitha Hardwick. Tabitha, this is my mother, Lilac Hearth."

I'd already called ahead to let Mom know Tabitha was tagging along to dinner. I knew there would be plenty of food to go around, regardless, but Mom appreciated a little heads-up. I also wanted to fill her in on the investigation into Aunt Lavender's abduction. As Lavender's younger—and only—sister, Mom was just as eager to get answers.

"It's lovely to meet you. Welcome to my home." Mom smiled as she shook Tabitha's hand. "I hope you like butternut squash!"

Tabitha smiled. "I love it."

"Good, because I've made at least a hundred of these little raviolis and stuffed them to the gills with the stuff!" Mom laughed and steered Tabitha toward the kitchen.

Mom didn't know a stranger. She was gracious and loving to everyone she met, and always willing to lend a helping hand to anyone in need. She wasn't as eccentric as her older sister, but she maintained a handful of hobbies, and often had her thoughts in two places at once.

Behind me, the front door opened and my brother's twins, Emme and Ruby, burst into the living room in a flurry of pink rain jackets and boots and little blonde pigtails. "Selene!"

My nieces were five years old and supernova explosions of energy.

Selene yowled and pounced to make a quick exit, disappearing up the stairs while the girls squealed with excitement and followed her, stumbling on the stairs as they tried to catch up.

"Be careful, girls." Cheyenne entered the foyer and shook her head with exasperation, rolling her eyes. "I swear, sometimes I don't even know what to do with them."

"Bottle up all that energy and sell it," my mother quipped.

Cheyenne's eyes twinkled with amusement. "I wish."

"They were chasing Selene," my mom explained.

"Oh no." Cheyenne's lips formed a pout. "Poor Selene. I hope she finds a good hiding spot before the twins try to stuff her into some of their baby doll clothes again."

I scoffed, laughing. "I'm sure she can handle it, the little drama queen that she is." I gestured to Tabitha. "Cheyenne, this is Tabitha Hardwick. Tabitha, this is my sister-in-law, Cheyenne."

Cheyenne's eyes widened into blossoming recognition. She blinked as if she were seeing a mirage in the desert and trying to figure out if it was real or not. Her jaw slackened and then hung open until it almost came unhinged.

"*Tabitha Hardwick*? As in *the* Tabitha Hardwick?"

Tabitha chuckled. Her expression was warm with amusement. "That's what I've been told."

"What are you doing here?" Cheyenne gawked.

"Wow. Most people just start with a 'nice to meet you,'" I teased.

Cheyenne squeezed her eyes shut, shook her head, opened her eyes again, and placed her palms on either side of her face. "I'm sorry. I don't mean to sound rude. It's just, I'm a little starstruck." She stared at Tabitha as if she were an enigma suddenly coming to life. "I listen to your podcast *all* the time. Seriously. It's my go-to. I've read your book too!"

"It's always nice to meet a fan." There was a sense of kindness and patience woven into Tabitha's voice that suggested she dealt with this kind of behavior from people all the time.

"I can't believe you're really standing here," Cheyenne said, seemingly unable to stop herself from gushing.

"She's going to have dinner with us," I said.

"Really?" Cheyenne gaped.

"She's volunteered to help us in the search for Aunt Lavender," I added.

"That's so kind." Cheyenne smiled, then began smoothing her hands over the fabric of her gray cardigan, as though trying to iron out the slight wrinkles. Or maybe she was trying to wipe away a layer of nervous sweat.

Either way, I knew Cheyenne well enough by now

to know that she was trying to keep her composure but, on the inside, she was probably jumping up and down like a little kid on Christmas morning.

"What's all the excitement about?" My brother Evan appeared in the doorway. He wore a navy-blue sweater with the sleeves rolled up to the elbows, and a pair of well-worn jeans.

Evan was always the tallest person in the room, standing at six feet two inches. His short-cropped brown hair was clean cut as always, with subtle traces of gray starting to peek through. Evan didn't mind the gray, nor did he try to cover it up. He usually turned it into a joke, blaming it on the twins and their playful antics. "Those girls are going to make me gray before their next birthday," he'd say with a chuckle.

He was a remarkable father, a true natural. He would do anything for his daughters and jumped into the role of 'twin dad' without an ounce of reservation.

"Come on," Mom said, leading the way to the dining room. "Dinner is just about ready, and I've made a feast."

"What else is new," I said as I cut my mother a smile of approval.

"Something sure smells delicious," Tabitha said.

Mom gestured to the seat next to her. "Tabitha, you can sit here."

I watched Cheyenne's face fall when she realized that she wouldn't be sitting directly next to Tabitha, but instead on the other side of the table in her usual spot.

"Don't worry," I whispered as I slipped in behind her and tugged on the fleshy fold of her elbow. "You'll have plenty of time to talk her ear off before the night is over."

Cheyenne's eyes flashed in my direction, and she tried to give me an optimistic smile.

Evan wrangled the twins, while I helped Mom bring the food to the table. Within a few minutes we were all seated, and Mom began passing the serving bowls around, allowing Tabitha first dibs on each dish.

Tabitha gave my mom an approving nod a few minutes into the meal. "This is delicious, Lilac. You'll have to give me the recipe, assuming it's not top secret." She smiled as she lifted the napkin to her lips and dabbed at the edges of her mouth.

My mother's eyes lit up as if she'd just been given the biggest and most life-altering compliment in her entire life. "Do you enjoy cooking?"

Tabitha bobbed her head. "When I have time."

"I imagine that's in short supply, considering your ventures." Mom coiled her fingers around the stem of her wineglass.

"Very short," Tabitha agreed. "Though, I can't complain. I've eaten many wonderful meals in my travels."

"Ooh! I can just imagine. What's your favorite?"

"Just about anything that comes from Italy," Tabitha

teased with a soft chuckle. "I think I must have been an Italian pizza chef in another life."

Everyone laughed. Mom glanced at the plate of her homemade ravioli. "Well, now I'm doubly flattered by your compliment, if my own pasta can compete."

Tabitha cut into another ravioli, a bit of the squash spilling out onto the plate. "Most definitely! Perhaps you were Italian in another life, too."

Mom grinned. "I may just have some gelato in the freezer for dessert. The container states it's been imported from Italy. Sounds like Tabitha here can tell us if it's the real deal."

"Gelato?" Evan said, his eyes going wide. "You know, Mom, remember what Grandma used to say: Life is short, eat dessert first."

The twins sat up like a pair of lightning bolts. "Can we have dessert first?"

Cheyenne groaned. "Thanks a lot, babe." She shook her head and frowned at her girls. "Daddy is being a bad influence. Now come on." She pointed her fork in the direction of Ruby's untouched asparagus spears. "Eat up."

"I don't like green food." Ruby sulked, her little eyebrows knitting as she frowned.

"No one does, kid," Evan said.

Sometimes Evan could be a bit of a big kid himself.

"You're not helping." Cheyenne shot her husband an annoyed glance.

"What if I told you I added a little *magic* to the asparagus?" Mom asked, grinning at the girls as she leaned into the table. She wiggled her fingers as if magically peppering their food with something divine.

"What kind of magic?" Emme gave my mom a sideways, questioning glance.

Mom beamed at her grandbabies. "They'll make you run *extra* fast!"

Ruby picked up one of the spears, bypassing her fork, and chomped off the tip.

"Nice work," Cheyenne mouthed with relief to my mom.

"Speaking of magic," I offered, "Tabitha, Selene, and I have been working hard today at the library, studying up on spells and incantations we might be able to use to aid in finding Aunt Lavender."

Cheyenne's eyes popped and she glanced between me and Tabitha, chewing on a piece of her buttered bread. "Oh really?"

"We're making progress," Tabitha noted.

"That's amazing news." Mom placed her fingers to her collarbone. "We've been so worried about Lavender. I've been using divination efforts to try and find her but haven't been able to maintain a strong enough link to communicate with her."

"Well, I think Cora is onto something with her theory about this all relating back to the hunt for the Golden Lotus," Tabitha said. "If Lavender knew something about its location, it could be motive enough for someone to take her."

The more Tabitha explained her agenda and purpose, the more the mood around the table lifted, like a heavy fog finally clearing into a warm and sunny day. So far, she hadn't added any of her own theories, but there was something reassuring about her validation of the progress we'd made so far.

"We're also working on scheduling a meeting with Warden Quinton," I added.

"Oh?" My mother gave me a promising smile.

"She's supposed to be coming into town soon," I explained.

Mom clasped her hands together, her cheeks a flushed rosy color, a combination from the wine and her excitement for progress in solving her sister's disappearance.

"This is all wonderful news. I think it's cause to celebrate with a little bit of chocolate gelato!" Mom said, already getting up from her place at the table.

The twins' forks clattered to their plates. "Chocolate!" they squealed in unison.

MY HANDS WERE SUBMERGED under warm, soapy water.

I lifted a clean plate, turned the sink faucet to warm, and rinsed the suds off under the water.

My mom stood beside me, a towel in her hand. She swiped it across a large serving dish to dry it.

"Honey?"

"Hmm?" I asked without looking up.

"Where was Clint tonight?"

"Clint?" My heart drummed faster at the mention of his name. I lifted my gaze and turned my head toward my mother.

Her smile was maternal. "Yes, Clint, you remember —your boyfriend?"

"Oh." I frowned and settled my focus back on the dishes. "I didn't want to overwhelm you with too many guests."

"You know I wouldn't have been bothered by that." Mom picked up a wineglass and patted it dry.

"I know…" I trailed off, thinking of excuses to buy me time but they were all too lukewarm for my mother to believe.

"Is everything okay with you two?" The lilt in Mom's voice let me know that she was testing the waters to see how much I would admit to her.

"Everything's fine." My voice sounded stiffer than I wanted it to, so I padded it with a reassuring smile in my mother's direction.

She seemed satisfied by my claim for now. "That's great to hear. I really like Clint."

"I know you do."

"You should invite him for dinner next time. We'd love to see him again."

"Maybe next time," I said, then not to disappoint my mother any further, I forced an enthusiastic smile.

6

"*I* come bearing gifts."

I held up a piping-hot cup of coffee and slid it across the table to Tabitha.

Tabitha reached for it with a grateful smile, wrapping her hands around the mug. She drew it to her lips and took a dainty sip so as not to burn her tongue. "Mmm." She breathed out through her nose and closed her eyes. "You're a lifesaver."

"No problem." I pulled a seat out from underneath the tan-colored library table and parked myself in it. The morning sun was canary yellow, splashing a beam of warming light that filtered through the enormous floor-to-ceiling windows behind us.

"Where is *my* breakfast?" Selene asked, her grumpy morning voice in full effect. Her tail twitched before she coiled it around her backside.

"You already ate it, remember?" I rolled my eyes and

exchanged an amused smile with Tabitha that Selene thankfully didn't notice.

"That was *hours* ago," the cat replied with another tail flick.

I made a show of checking my watch. "It was exactly forty-five minutes ago."

Selene's glower grew darker.

Sighing, I reached into my purse and dug out a small bag of cat treats. I'd made a special trip to the pet store a few days ago to buy them. It was one more step in my slippery slide into becoming a full-blown cat lady, but I figured anything to keep the cat's blood sugars in check was worth it considering how cranky she could get.

I shook a few of the green pellets onto the table in front of her. "There. Happy now?"

Selene's eyes got huge as her whiskers twitched. "What are those?"

"Cat treats." I consulted the front of the package. "Says here they are roast chicken flavor."

Selene narrowed her eyes. "I ask for a tuna steak and she brings me chicken-flavored gravel."

"Beggars can't be choosers." I shrugged. "Besides, I can't bring tuna steaks into the library. You're lucky to get anything at all."

"I don't see why not," Selene said, still glaring at the cat treats like they might be radioactive.

"Well, food and drinks are generally frowned upon here," I said. "The only reason I could get the coffee in here is because Penny is at the front desk, and she likes me."

The cat snapped her tail again. "There's a simple solution, Cora. The Goddess blessed you with pockets for a reason."

"Oh, yeah, I'm sure no one would notice the ever-so-lovely scent of your fishy delights."

Selene lifted her chin, snubbing the treats alto-gether. "I happen to believe that tuna steaks smell *divine*."

I stuffed the bag back into my purse, leaving the cluster of treats on the table. "Eat them or not. I don't care."

The cat gave the treats another side-eye glance.

As the finicky feline contemplated her snack, I shifted my attention to Tabitha. I offered a sheepish smile by way of silent apology for the cat's antics, then cleared my throat. "Thanks for meeting us here so early."

Tabitha finished her sip of coffee and smiled. "It's no problem. I've always been an early bird."

"So." I straightened my posture and scooted the chair closer to the table. "Where should we start?"

"Well," Tabitha began, her smile uplifted. "I did a little digging into Salvatore Greco."

"Oh?" My eyebrows arched upward.

Tabitha nodded, glancing at some notes she'd jotted down in the notebook she'd had at Dragon's Gold the day before. "According to my research, he left every-thing to his nephew, Ernesto Greco."

Selene's ears perked as she slid me a knowing look.

Tabitha noticed, her eyes skirting between us. "I take it you already knew that?"

I glanced down at my coffee and nodded. "We aren't exactly on the best of terms with the nephew."

Tabitha set her notebook down on the table. "What happened?"

I propped one elbow up on the table and twisted a strand of my short hair around in my finger.

Selene, blunt as usual, cut straight to the point. "We got his wife thrown into the pokey for offing good old Sal."

Tabitha's eyes widened, almost like she wasn't sure whether to believe the cat or not.

"It's a little more involved than that," I said, shooting Selene an annoyed look.

Selene swiped at the treats with one paw, managing to fling one off the table. Amusement sparked in her eyes, and she quickly made a game of it, knocking the others off in turn.

Tabitha didn't seem to notice. "I think we need to speak with Ernesto. He lives here in Winterspell, correct?"

My gaze snapped away from the obnoxious cat. "You want to go talk to him?"

"Why not?" Tabitha's expression was casual.

I exchanged a wary glance with Selene.

'I don't know. I mean—well, I suppose. I just don't know how helpful he'll be, especially to me and Selene.'

I pinched my lips together and frowned down at my coffee. My stomach felt unsettled at the idea of talking to Ernesto, especially in person.

"You want to find your Aunt Lavender, right?" Tabitha leaned forward with an expectant gaze burning into me.

My chin nodded up and down. "Yes. Of course."

"Then we have to start somewhere. Perhaps Ernesto knows something about the missing pages. If we don't explore all angles, then we're never going to get anywhere. If I've learned one thing from treasure hunting, it's that the more risks you take, the better the rewards are in the end."

I traced the logo lettering on the front of my coffee cup, knowing she was right.

"All right. Let's do it. The sooner we find Lavender, the better."

Closure, above all else, was the thing I hunted most.

"Yeesh, he's really let the place go, huh?" Selene peered out the window with a look of reservation on her face at the abandoned-looking property.

I gave Ernesto's front yard an apprehensive scan.

The blinds were drawn, shut tight. The grass was high and looked like it hadn't been mowed in several weeks. The flower bed lining the front of the house was peppered with weeds and the flowers were wilted and dry, looking in desperate need of water.

It stood in stark contrast to the other homes in the exclusive Rolling Pine Hills. The last time we'd seen it, there was no difference between it and the carefully cultivated lawns of its neighbors. It was one of those housing developments where one had to get approval from the homeowners' association before repainting their house or ordering a new front door. Nothing could clash. There wasn't room for individualism among the upper-middle-class McMansions.

Tabitha took it in, then marched up the driveway with purposeful strides. Selene and I exchanged a cautious look and followed her up to the front door. Tabitha pressed the doorbell before taking a step back to wait.

My heart lodged itself in my throat.

A shadow moved behind the glass panes on the door, but it took a long moment before the deadbolt clicked, and for a moment, I wasn't sure if the person on the other side was unlocking or locking it in place.

"Mr. Greco?" Tabitha called. "Please, we'd like to speak with you."

I held my breath as Ernesto cracked the door open, craning just his head out to give the three of us a guarded stare. Beyond Ernesto's shoulder the interior lay in darkness.

When his eyes landed on me and Selene, recognition widened in his eyes, and he opened the door an inch more. "Wait a second. I know you."

"Hello, Ernesto." I gave him a timid wave.

Ernesto blinked at me, his features etched in surprise. His hair was a tousled mess on top of his head. He reached up a self-conscious hand to plaster it back down to his head as much as he could. He wore a white T-shirt and gray jogging pants.

"I hope we didn't wake you," I said.

"No." He shook his head and glanced over his shoulder before returning his gaze to me. "No, you didn't."

Tabitha took a confident step forward. Her shoulders formed a straight, impeccable line. "Ernesto, my name is Tabitha Hardwick. We're looking for information about the disappearance of Lavender Hearth. If we might be so bold as to ask for a few minutes of your time, we'd love to pick your brain about it."

I scratched my temple with my fingernail and looked down as Tabitha took the reins of the conversation.

Ernesto shifted his weight, eyeballing us each in turn, though his gaze tended to linger on Tabitha. Not that I could blame him. She oozed confidence and her own brand of alluring mystery. She was dressed in black leather boots and a leather jacket over a black dress in a jersey knit fabric that complemented her silvery-mauve hair. Her eye makeup was smoky, and she had on the same red lipstick she'd had on the day before, when we first met. Her wrists were decorated in flashy bracelets that made a clanking sound whenever she moved her arms.

Smiling, Tabitha pounced. "Can we come inside?"

"Oh, uh, yeah." Ernesto shifted his weight, looking awkward as he opened the door the rest of the way. He backed into it and gestured for us to enter. "Come on in."

His eyes were still fixed on Tabitha as we slid past him into the foyer.

When Ernesto fumbled to turn on the lights, it became clear that Michelle was the muscle behind the household chores, and in her absence, the home's interior had fallen into the same sad state as the landscaping.

Selene placed a paw over her tiny, pink nose. "Yuck," she hissed. "It smells gross in here."

"Don't be rude," I whispered through the side of my mouth, hoping that she'd heard me, but that Ernesto had not.

We followed Ernesto deeper into the house. A sting of pity hit me in the chest as he scrambled to pick up some of the mess. Piles of laundry cluttered the couch, leaving only one seat free, and that cushion was a mess of crumbs. The coffee table was piled with discarded pizza boxes and takeout soda cups.

"Sorry," he said, his voice a little shaky. "I've been busy lately and haven't had much time to keep the house in order. I'm trying to deal with my uncle's inheritance money, and I'm bogged down with selling his estate. Some days I feel like I'm drowning in paperwork and red tape. I had no idea how much detail went into managing an estate like his."

He tossed the clothes into a white plastic laundry basket beside the TV. Console controllers and a pile of video games were sitting on the floor next to the TV stand.

Ernesto gave Tabitha a pained half smile. "On top of it all, my ex-wife was more of the neat freak than I am."

He'd addressed the elephant in the room in a roundabout way.

"That's okay." Tabitha was breezy, her eyes animated. "We won't keep you long. We just have a few questions."

Ernesto clasped his hands together and gave her a nod. "Okay. Yeah. Um. What's up?"

My eyes roamed around the room. I caught a glimpse of the kitchen from the angle where I stood. The sink was piled high with several inches of dirty dishes, and various takeout boxes took up all the space on the counters. I didn't regret my part in sending his wife—or, ex-wife, as he'd said—to prison. But I couldn't help but feel a little bad to see Ernesto's pain so evidently on display.

Tabitha's face was all business, clutter or not. Her

eyes locked on Ernesto. "I'm sorry for your loss," she began. "I imagine what you're going through isn't easy."

Ernesto gave an awkward nod. "Thanks."

"You said you're managing Salvatore's estate now," Tabitha continued, not missing a beat. "Would that also include his rare book trade?"

Ernesto tore his gaze away from Tabitha and looked at me. "Is this about … Michelle?" He nearly stumbled over his wife's name.

Michelle Greco had killed Sal after he caught her trying to steal Obin's Odyssey to sell and clear their personal debt.

"No," I answered. "At least, not directly. We want to find your uncle's notes on one of the books he had in his possession."

I left off the part about it being the one Michelle wanted to steal. Ernesto likely knew the details, so there was no point in dredging it up again.

Ernesto exhaled as he reached up to rub the back of his neck. "I haven't done much with any of that yet." He dropped his hand, then looked at Tabitha. He straightened his posture a little and attempted to suck in his gut. "If you want, I could let you into his house to take a look for yourselves. You probably know better than I do what you're looking for."

Tabitha's smile dripped with appeal. "You would let us do that?"

Ernesto shoved his hands into the pockets of his jogger pants and shrugged. "Sure, why not?"

"That's very generous of you," I said from a few steps behind Tabitha.

Ernesto met my gaze. There was a solemnness in his eyes that gave me a trace of guilt. "No problem." His voice was low, and he didn't keep his eyes on me for long.

"We'd *love* to take the opportunity to do that," Tabitha chimed in, as if she was afraid that if we hesitated any longer that Ernesto might change his mind.

Ernesto's eyes trailed bleakly over his messy living room. "If you can just give me a few minutes—"

"We could meet you over there," Tabitha suggested.

I winced, hoping she wasn't seeming too overeager to Ernesto.

"That works," Ernesto said, his face showing relief. "I just need to get changed first. Do you remember where it is?" His eyes cut to me.

"Yes," I nodded.

Tabitha clapped her hands together with a gleam of approval flashing in her eyes. "Wonderful. We'll see you over there!"

HALF AN HOUR LATER, Ernesto led us up the long staircase inside his uncle Sal's estate. "The library is at the top of the landing and at the end of the hallway," he explained, though we already knew. "I'll wait down-stairs. I might load up a few more boxes while you look around."

"Thank you, Ernesto." Tabitha flashed our host a winning smile.

He headed down the stairs and we went forward to Ernesto's personal library.

Memories of my fight with Michelle flashed like snapshots of a camera in my mind. Selene was unchar-acteristically quiet, too. Without her help that night, I wasn't sure either of us would be alive today.

Tabitha didn't know about that night and moved through the hallway with her signature confidence. "This one?" she asked, turning back to look at me.

I shook my head to clear my thoughts, then gave her a quick nod. "That's the one."

The library appeared more or less just as Sal had left it. It smelled of paper, cigars, brandy, and old books. Rows and rows of books lined the two-story library like a maze of knowledge, imagination, and indulgence.

It felt like an impossible challenge to be able to investigate the wide spectrum of books in here.

I shoved aside that overwhelming sensation and reminded myself that I wasn't alone in this and that I had plenty of help for the cause.

Selene snapped to attention, wasting no time as she jumped up onto the large mahogany desk.

A thin film of dust spread across the elegant wood

surface and the handful of items left behind. I ran the tip of my fingers down the spine of a pine-green book set to one side. There wasn't a title embossed in the soft leather, and when I lifted the cover, I realized it was a journal of sorts.

"This place is pretty incredible," Tabitha said, still taking it all in as she circled the perimeter.

"I think I might have found something," I said as I flipped through the pages. There were careful notes detailing each day. "It looks like Sal kept a journal."

"Oh?" Tabitha's voice pitched with interest.

The first few entries I scanned were fairly dull. But on the third page, I caught a few sentences mentioning a rare book he'd acquired. It wasn't Obin's Odyssey, but another tome. With a spark of excitement, I anxiously flipped ahead, using the dates to find the location of where he might have come into possession of Obin's tome.

My heart thumped when I hit pay dirt.

"You guys … look at this."

"What is it?" Selene jumped onto the desk and leaned forward to poke her head closer to the ledger.

"There are some notes about Obin's Odyssey," I explained, my eyes desperately reading all the notes two times through. When I was sure I hadn't misunderstood, I looked up and met Tabitha's gaze. "It says the book was in pristine condition when Sal acquired it."

Tabitha tapped a finger against the corner of her

mouth. "So, the pages were removed somewhere between the time Sal received the book, but before Lavender took it?"

I nodded. "His notes are meticulous. I saw a few other listings and they all mentioned if there was any damage to the books he accepted or sold."

Tabitha's eyes narrowed into concentration, and she nodded. "Interesting. Does it say where he acquired the book?"

Frowning, I looked down at the ledger. "No," I replied after a pause. "Which is weird, because most of the other notes include that information."

"Humph." Selene sat down abruptly. "Too bad the old geezer had to go and get himself murdered."

"Selene…"

Tabitha took a photo of the pages with the camera on her cellphone.

It was progress.

My heart galloped.

We now had something to work off of, and we had only just arrived. If only the rest of the investigation could go this smoothly.

Fingers crossed.

7

"The first thing we need to do is find out *who* would have access to Sal's rare book collection between those two time frames," Tabitha said, tapping her perfect, teal nails against the front of the ledger.

"Agreed," I replied. "Knowing the book was tampered with after Sal acquired it means we have that definitive timeline to investigate. We need to take that lead and run with it."

"Let's keep looking," Selene said, hopping down from the desk.

Tabitha pocketed her phone. She'd photographed the pages of the most recent of Sal's entries. She followed Selene to the bookcase opposite the desk. Something caught her eye, and she reached up to grab a book. Selene slithered around a bronze sculpture to avoid Tabitha's hand and bumped into a stack of books.

Recoiling, the cat's ears went flat. "What the heck—these ones aren't real," she said.

"What do you mean?" Tabitha stood on her tiptoes and touched the books in question. With a little gasp, she pulled the stack down, only to find the whole thing lifted away in one piece and was, in fact, hollow. "It's a prop? Why would he need prop books?" She cast a glance around. "It's not like he's hurting for reading material."

"There's a cut in the wood," Selene said. She placed a paw on the shelf where the fake books had been stacked.

At her cautious touch, the bookcase shuddered to life and began sliding backward, farther into the wall.

With a yowling cry, Selene dove off the moving bookcase, narrowly missing Tabitha. The bookcase disappeared into the dark, and then soft lights popped on, illuminating a pathway.

"What in the world?"

I jumped and turned at the sound of Ernesto's voice behind us.

His jaw hung open, his eyes wide.

Tabitha glanced between him and the ominous pathway. "You didn't know about this?"

Ernesto took a guarded step forward as if he was afraid that he was going to fall through a trap door or something. He shook his head. "I've never seen this in my life."

"Interesting..." Tabitha trailed off in a low, spectating voice. "Well, shall we?" she asked.

"You're kidding!" Selene said, before glancing up at me. "She's kidding, right?"

With a laugh, Tabitha strode into the strange cave. "Trust me, this is a cakewalk compared to my normal gigs. I don't even see any spiderwebs!"

Selene shuddered. "Yeah, it's all fun and games until you trip another booby trap and iron spikes start closing in around you."

I looked from Selene to Tabitha's back, and then drew in a breath.

"You're seriously going into that death trap?" Selene asked, a note of panic in her voice.

"You know, for someone who is supposedly invincible, you sure are a chicken sometimes." I smiled and took a step into the hall.

Selene growled. "Okay, that's it! I'm not going to let you two get all the glory."

Tabitha ignited some kind of magical ball of light, amplifying the smaller lights on the sides of the hall. We walked about twenty paces before we reached a door. Tabitha twisted the knob and smiled. "No lock."

"Stand back, Cora," Selene warned. "This is probably where the trap is!"

I rolled my eyes and nodded to Tabitha. "I'm good to go if you are."

Tabitha opened the door and slipped inside, taking her orb of light with her. Ernesto and I followed after her and only after confirming we hadn't died, Selene joined us.

"Up there." I pointed above Ernesto's head. "There's a dangling string with a light bulb attached to the ceiling."

Ernesto glanced up, lifted his arm, and gave the string a gentle tug. The light clicked on a moment later, making a sharp crackling sound as it buzzed to life.

Tabitha extinguished her magical light and slowly spun on her heels to take in our new surroundings. From the look of things, we were in yet another library, though this one was a mere fraction of the size of the one we'd just left.

"Wow," I whispered as I considered the shelves. The room was utilitarian and plain, especially in comparison to the main library. It was more of a vault or storage room.

"It's temperature controlled," Ernesto said, touching a thermostat on an adjacent wall. "It says it's seventy-two degrees in here."

"Any idea what we're looking at here?" Tabitha asked him.

"I didn't even know this was here," he replied. "I'd guess it's where Uncle Sal kept his rarest books. These ones all look really old."

Tabitha nodded as she approached a shelf. "I agree. This is probably where he hid his most expensive and valuable collection."

Selene lifted her chin. "You're welcome. Seriously, what would you do without me?"

The chime of a ringtone sounded, and Ernesto jolted. He dug his phone out of his pocket, then quickly excused himself, saying he needed to take the call.

As soon as he was out of earshot, Tabitha turned toward us, her brow furrowed. "How could he not have known about this place?"

I shook my head. "I don't know. From what we heard about Ernesto, he wasn't into any of his uncle's business. Sal was grooming him to take over his place on the Arcane Council, but it doesn't sound like Ernesto took it too seriously. Either he figured he could skate by on his uncle's reputation alone, or he thought he had time to learn later. No one expected Sal to die when he did."

Tabitha's frown deepened. "I just don't see how he couldn't know even the basics."

I shrugged. "It's probably for the best. If Ernesto had known about this place, then his wife, er, ex-wife, Michelle, would have too. She would have cleaned this place out and sold the entire lot of it to fund her shopping habit."

Tabitha rolled her fingers through the air. "Okay. Rewind. What are you talking about?"

Selene and I quickly caught her up on the events of Sal's murder, including the confrontation we'd had with Michelle in the hallway not too far from the library's doors. When we finished, Tabitha's expression was more skeptical than ever. "Do you think there's a chance Sal *purposely* kept the vault from Ernesto?"

"I—I don't know."

Tabitha licked her lips. I could practically see the gears turning in her mind. "If Sal's own nephew didn't know about the vault, then how could anyone else have known about it?"

"Maybe Sal didn't have the book in the vault at the time the pages were ripped out," Selene suggested. "He had it out in the main library when he showed it to Lavender. The day she swiped it."

I inclined my head toward the cat. "Very true."

"Or maybe someone *did* have access to the vault, and we just don't know who that is yet," Tabitha countered.

"I do know that Sal used to open his personal library to university students as well as other researchers," I mentioned. "That's how Lavender and Selene met Sal in the first place."

I glanced down at Selene who nodded. "Yep. That's right. Lavender used to do research here. She built a relationship with Sal over the years as she visited more and more frequently."

Ernesto reappeared in the frame of the vault's doorway. "Everything going okay down here?"

"We're just talking," Tabitha said quickly.

Ernesto wrung his hands. "I remembered something that might be worth mentioning."

Tabitha gave him an expectant glance.

"Uncle Sal had a maid," Ernesto continued.

"Mrs. White in the kitchen, with the candelabra!" Selene said.

I slapped a hand over my face.

"Did she have access to the whole house?" Tabitha asked, ignoring Selene.

Ernesto scratched his fingers across the jawline of his dark stubble. "He had one full-time person who looked after the place. She lives here in town. I haven't had the heart to fire her, so she still comes to the house once a week to clean."

"Hmm." This seemed odd to me, given the fact that there was a layer of dust on the library desk where I'd found the ledger.

"There isn't much for her to do, of course, now that the house is unoccupied," Ernesto added, his voice rising higher and getting faster. "Listen, I hate to be rude and ask you to wrap this up, but I need to get going."

"Of course." I gave him a polite smile.

"Can we get the maid's name and address before we leave?" Tabitha asked.

Ernesto gave her a funny look, licked his lips, and nodded. "Yeah. Uh-huh. Sure."

We walked up the stairs, closed the vault to its original, concealed state, and watched as Ernesto jotted down the address for us from a pen and pad in Sal's office.

Then we followed Ernesto as he escorted us to the

front of the house, shuffled us out the large double doors leading onto the porch of the property, and waved goodbye to us as we climbed into my car.

"Now what?" I sighed, putting my car into gear.

Tabitha held up the paper with the maid's information and fanned it through the air, pinching it between her thumb and index finger. Her eyes gleaming, she declared, "*Now* we go and pay Ms. Bernadette Wise, the maid, a visit."

8

*B*ernadette Wise lived in a modest town house a few blocks from Winterspell's main street. The development was fairly new, and the rows of homes looked well maintained, each with its own neat postage-stamp yard. Bernadette's unit was sandwiched between two others and her porch was covered in planters and flowerpots. A wooden welcome sign was mounted to the exterior wall to the right of her front door.

As we got out of the car, dogs in the unit next to Bernadette's jumped in the front window, barking like mad. Selene's tail went rigid as she stared them down. "You sure you want a piece of this, mutts?"

"Selene, we don't have time for this," I told her, resisting the urge to nudge her forward with the toe of my suede boot.

Tabitha chuckled softly as she passed us on the sidewalk. "I like your spirit, Selene."

"At least *someone* appreciates me," the cat said, giving me a quick scowl before scampering ahead to keep pace with Tabitha.

"Give it a week," I muttered.

Tabitha strode up the steps and pressed the doorbell without hesitation. Mentally, I was still trying to figure out our best *in* with Salvatore's former maid. As the chime rang through the town house, I cut a quick look over at Tabitha. Her profile was set with determination, but she kept her posture relaxed.

Before I could ask her for the game plan, the front door opened and a woman with dark brown eyes and wiry, short brown hair peeked through the slit. "Can I help you?" she asked with a trace of an accent, although I couldn't place it.

"Hello," Tabitha replied, flashing her winning smile. "We are looking for Bernadette Wise. Does she live here?"

The woman's eyes narrowed. "Who's asking?"

"My name is Tabitha Hardwick. This is Cora Hearth and her familiar, Selene." Tabitha gestured to each of us in turn. "We were given your name by Ernesto Greco. We have some questions about Salvatore Greco, if you wouldn't mind."

At the mention of Salvatore's name, the woman's eyes softened. "Oh? What about him?"

"Are you Bernadette?" Tabitha lifted her eyebrows.

The woman hesitated before admitting, "Yes, I am." She glanced over her shoulder, then took a step back and opened the door wider. "Please, come inside. I've just put on the kettle. We can have some tea."

"Thank you. That's very kind," I replied.

We went inside the town house and followed Bernadette to her kitchen. She wasn't much taller than me, but where I had more of a pear-shaped figure, hers was more of an apple. I wasn't great at guessing age, but I imagined she was somewhere in her late forties, maybe early fifties, judging by the fine lines at her eyes and the silver streaks in her otherwise dark hair.

She busied herself in the kitchen, asking us each for our preference in teas. Next to the kettle she had a wooden box filled with dozens of tea bags. Either she was used to entertaining, or she just had a lot of favorite varieties.

Once we were settled at the dining table adjacent to the kitchen, she wrapped her fingers around her steaming mug and glanced up at us. "What would you like to know about Mr. Greco?"

"Did you know about his rare book vault?" Tabitha asked.

I blinked, struggling to keep my expression neutral. I hadn't quite expected her to swan dive right into the deep end.

Lines formed between Bernadette's brows as she considered the question. I couldn't tell if she was caught off guard by the question, annoyed by it, or genuinely confused. "I'm sorry, but what do you mean?"

Tabitha kept her eyes on Bernadette. "The vault in Sal's library."

Bernadette shook her head and frowned. "How was it you knew Sal?"

"We're friends of Ernesto's," Tabitha said, not missing a beat. "We're trying to help him figure out a few things involving the estate."

"Oh." Bernadette pressed her lips together for a moment. "I see. I guess that means he's getting serious about selling it, then?"

Worry flickered in the woman's eyes as she stared down at the contents of her mug. My heart went out to her. It wouldn't be too hard to find another house-keeping job in Winterspell, but there weren't many estates like Salvatore's. And while I didn't know how much Salvatore paid her, I imagined it would take several new contracts to make up the lost income.

"Have you heard about the vault before?" Tabitha asked.

Bernadette's shoulders wilted as she drew out a long, deep breath. "I knew about it."

Tabitha slid me a quick glance, her eyes alight.

Bernadette continued. "I found the secret panel on accident one day when I was dusting in the library. When I asked Mr. Greco if he wanted me to tidy up inside, he told me not to worry about it."

"So, he didn't seem upset that you'd found it?" I asked.

Bernadette shrugged. "He didn't seem to be."

"He must have trusted you a lot," Tabitha said, offering a kindhearted smile.

"I worked for Mr. Greco for a long time," Bernadette replied, a new emotion in her eyes. She lifted her mug and took a tentative sip.

"Does it strike you as odd that Ernesto didn't know about the vault?" Tabitha asked, leaning her head to one side.

Bernadette set her mug down. She considered Tabitha and me for a moment.

"Come on," Selene said, "spill the tea, as the kids say."

Bernadette glanced down at her mug, her brow furrowed once more. "I—I'm sorry, you want me to spill my tea?"

Selene groaned and jumped down from the table. "Never mind."

"We're trying to figure out why Sal wouldn't have told Ernesto about the vault," I said, quickly trying to cover the rude behavior of my familiar. "We found it this afternoon and Ernesto seemed quite taken aback by it, that's all."

"I see." Bernadette nodded, but a hint of suspicion lingered in her dark eyes. "It doesn't surprise me, to tell you the truth. Sal was probably waiting for Ernesto to take things more seriously, though if you ask me, that was never going to happen."

"Do you know if Salvatore had a backup plan? Someone else he would have trusted to take over the business some day? In case Ernesto never came around?"

Bernadette shook her head as a sad smile tugged at her lips. "No. Sal was always an optimist." The smile faded. "I've seen Ernesto a few times since his uncle's passing. He's not a bad man. He's kept me employed, even though the estate is abandoned. But I doubt he will ever follow in his uncle's footsteps. I imagine the estate will be sold sooner rather than later now that he's started clearing it out. For a time, I thought he would move in, but it's too large for him. He doesn't have the skills needed to maintain it. Perhaps if Michelle were still in the picture…"

Bernadette's words trailed off and her grip on the mug tightened.

"Do you know anything about Obin's Odyssey?" Tabitha asked, shifting gears before we lost Bernadette to reverie.

"I have no idea what you're talking about," Bernadette said with a soft laugh. "I'm assuming it's a book, but anything like that was above my pay grade." She smiled and relaxed slightly. "If you needed to know which houseplants need tending to on which days or where to find the feather duster, I'd be a fountain of information!"

Tabitha and I offered Bernadette a polite, grateful smile.

"Salvatore used to invite students and researchers to his library. Is that right?" Tabitha asked.

Bernadette nodded. "That's right."

"Did he keep a log or a sign-in sheet for those visits?"

Bernadette shook her head. "No, nothing like that. Those who had permission knew when they were allowed to have access. They also knew when to leave."

"Did the people who had access ever take any of the books home with them?" I asked.

"Not that I can recall." Bernadette rubbed her jawline as she thought about it. "Sal didn't normally let anyone leave the house with any books. Anything that was read or searched through happened in the library and was put back before the guest left the house. I don't even think Sal allowed anyone to take anything out of the main library, much less the secret one."

Bernadette stopped, swallowed hard, and glanced between us with a wrinkle in her forehead. "I'm sorry I can't offer more assistance. I wish I could."

"You've been very helpful," I replied. "Thank you for your time."

Bernadette's eyes twinkled as they met with mine and the side of her lip curved into a slight smile. "You're welcome. And please, tell Ernesto I'm available to help if he should need anything during the transition. Maybe he could even put in a word for me with the new owners once he sells."

I nodded. "We'll be sure to pass that along to him."

"Thank you."

"I HAVE A THEORY," Tabitha announced that afternoon, as we sat around a table in Dragon's Gold Coffee. "Although it might be an unpopular opinion."

I set my latte aside. "Okay?"

"What if Ernesto is playing dumb about all this?" she asked. "What if he's just pretending like he doesn't know anything, so no one suspects him? I mean, we already know his wife, or ex-wife, was planning on scamming Salvatore. What if she wasn't working alone? What if she's just the one who got caught?"

With a shake of my head, I leaned back in my seat, one hand still wrapped around my cup. "Michelle was stealing the books so she could leave Ernesto. They weren't in on it together."

Selene paused her grooming session long enough to agree with me. "Besides, when we caught Michelle red-handed, she wasn't in the secret book vault. If she knew about it, that would have been her first stop."

"Ernesto didn't need to scam Salvatore or steal from him. He was already set to inherit everything for doing absolutely nothing. He just had to sit back and wait, and all the riches would come to him in time."

Tabitha rubbed her temples and sighed. "Right. Sorry. That was a rather dumb theory."

I smiled. "Don't worry about it. Selene and I have just already been on this particular merry-go-round."

"We can rule out Michelle *and* Ernesto as far as I'm concerned," Selene added before casually lifting a paw to resume her bath.

A dismal aura fell over the table, hanging over us like a cloaking fog.

My phone buzzed against the surface of the table and the screen lit up. I glanced over at it and winced. "It's Clint."

Tabitha took a deep breath and planted her palms on the top of the table to support herself as she stood. "I think I'm going to head back to my hotel. A jog would do me some good. Clear my mind. Can we pick up again in the morning?"

"Of course. Have a good night."

Once Tabitha left, I glanced over at Selene. "I hope she doesn't give up on us."

The cat rubbed her paw over her whiskers, smoothing them back. "If she gives up that easily, then who needs her."

I tried to smile, but as my gaze followed the path she'd cut on her way out of the coffee shop, I couldn't fully release the tension growing in my chest.

9

"*T*hank you for meeting me here," Clint said, offering a warm smile as I slid into the seat across from him. It looked like he'd snagged the last available booth at Elephant's Palace, the local Indian restaurant. He wore a blue sweater and slacks and his face appeared freshly shaved, without a hint of a five-o'clock shadow, though it was nearing seven.

I attempted a smile, though it felt stiff. "No problem."

"I was scared there for a second when you weren't answering my texts," Clint added as he handed me a menu.

"I've just been busy, that's all." I set the menu aside and shrugged out of my coat. "It wasn't intentional."

"Look, Cora, I want to clear the air between us."

I grabbed my menu. "Let's order first. I don't want to keep the kitchen waiting. It looks like they're busy."

Clint opened his mouth but thought better of whatever he'd been about to say, and picked up his menu. "Right. Of course. What looks good?"

We both knew what we'd order. I'd been a regular customer of the restaurant for years, and while Clint was newer in town, he was the kind who stayed latched onto something once he found what he liked. But we went through the motions, discussing a few options. It was like some kind of game, or a play.

When our server came to take our order, we exchanged a smile, as each ordered just what the other knew they would.

His smile melted me every time. I didn't want to have the conversation I knew we needed to have. We were from two different worlds. For a little while, I'd thought we might have a chance at meeting in the middle, but after the disastrous dinner at his mother's house, that illusion was shattered. I didn't fit into his world, and he was all but ready to abandon mine.

We tried to make small talk while we waited for our meals to arrive. The hum of conversation from our neighboring tables provided a distraction from the long pauses that we kept tripping over.

After our server dropped off our entrees, Clint cleared his throat and broached the subject again. "I know I dropped quite a bombshell the other day. In hindsight, I wish I had taken a few more days to sort through my options on my own before laying it out the way I did. Right now, things feel unsteady, and I shouldn't have thrown that on you, especially with everything you've got going on, with your aunt and all."

"It's okay." I tore off a corner of garlic naan and dipped it into the excess sauce along the edge of my plate. "We should be able to talk to each other about anything, even when things are a bit chaotic and unsettled."

"You're right. I want that, too." Clint bobbed his head. "But still, I can't help but feel like I spooked you."

Sighing, I set the naan aside and met his dark brown eyes. They were warm, almost glowing, under the lamp hanging over our booth. They'd been the first thing I noticed about him, back on the night we met. The whole thing had been so random. He'd gone from a visitor, stopping in my candle shop to buy a gift for his estranged mother, to a murder suspect, to my friend, to my boyfriend, all in such a short window of time.

My feelings for him were so strong, it seemed like we'd known each other far longer. Which only made it harder to think about it all fading away. Like some sort of dream. Would I look back on this relationship, years from now, and wonder if it even happened at all?

"I'm not really sure what to say, Clint. I can't ask you to give up your inheritance for me. And at the same time, I'm not willing to jump into something solely so you can keep it." I paused, taking a moment to consider my words carefully. "I really like you, and I don't want to lose you, but I have to protect myself.

I've been through one divorce, and it was one of the worst experiences of my life. I can't go through that again. I couldn't take another heartbreak like that one."

Clint reached across the table for my hand. "Cora, I'm not going to hurt you."

"I know you don't want to, but you can't guarantee things would work out. We're only just getting to know one another." My voice sounded hollow. "Marriage is a big step. A big deal. Even if we got to that place, somewhere down the line, I don't want to say yes, all the while wondering in the back of my head if it's for the right reasons."

Clint's grip on my hand loosened and he sagged back. "You really think I'm capable of that? This isn't some kind of trick, Cora. All I'm trying to do is make the right decision."

"I know." My throat constricted. "And all I'm saying is that you need to make that decision for yourself. Take me out of the equation."

Clint's brows lifted. "So, you want to end things?"

The words stung, like tiny little pinpricks straight into my heart. "It's not what I want. If a week ago someone told me we'd be having this conversation, I would have laughed in their face. I was so sure that this was going to work."

Clint made a frustrated little growl as he reached for his drink. "Nothing has to change, Cora. Can't you just forget what my mother said?"

I met his gaze. His eyes were wide and desperate. Sadly, I shook my head. "No. I can't."

"This is probably a stupid question, but there's no way you would consider moving to Chicago?"

I shook my head, my gaze falling to my nearly full plate, the piece of naan nearly drowned as it lay submerged in the sauce. "I'm really sorry, but no. My family is here. My business. Leanna."

"And you don't want to do long distance?" Clint asked.

I arched a brow, glancing up at him. "Do you?"

His expression crumpled again. "No."

"Listen, we don't have to decide on this tonight," I said, trying to infuse some sort of hope into my tone. "I think, for now, we each should focus on our own lives. Let this marinate a little longer. You've got your mother to tend to. I'm in the thick of things with Tabitha. Once we find Aunt Lavender I'll have more bandwidth for these kinds of decisions, okay?"

Clint nodded, but his attempt at a smile fell flat. "You're right. We can enjoy the time we do have."

The words did nothing to clear the dread swirling in my stomach. We picked at our meals a little longer, before asking for two takeout containers. Clint insisted on paying the check, as he was the one who'd invited me out.

When the bill was settled, he escorted me outside and offered to walk me to my car, though it was only a few yards away. I noticed his BMW parked three cars away. We paused at my front bumper, each holding our box of leftovers. "Well, good night," I said. "Thanks again for dinner. This will make a good lunch tomorrow, even though Selene will undoubtedly complain about the smell."

Clint chuckled. "I wouldn't expect anything less from her royal highness."

I smiled. "Don't let her catch you calling her that. With my luck, she'd insist on me buying her a tiara, and we both know cubic zirconia wouldn't cut it."

Clint's smile widened. "Noted."

He pulled me in for a quick embrace, his lip gracing the side of my cheek before he released me. "Good night, Cora."

"Good night, Clint."

IT WAS THURSDAY NIGHT, so after leaving Elephant's Palace, I headed up the road a few blocks and pulled into the parking lot outside Merlin's Well. I knew that my best friend, Leanna, would be inside, sitting at the bar, scoping the place for a handsome hunk to buy her a drink on Ladies' Night.

Sure enough, a smile spread across my face as I pulled into the parking lot and my headlights traced across her sedan. I parked and hurried inside, my hands shoved into my coat pockets as I walked against the wind.

Leanna was sitting at the bar closest to the door, a pink cocktail in one hand, as she chatted with Gerry, the Scottish barkeep and proprietor of the tavern. The place was buzzing with patrons, some shooting pool and playing darts, others dancing on the cleared-out space in front of the jukebox, while others nursed drinks in darkened corners.

Leanna caught sight of me and instantly brightened. "Hey, you! What are you doing here?"

"I came to see you. Looks like I got here before some tall, dark, and handsome swept you away." I grinned as I hauled myself up onto one of the tall stools dotting the long, wooden bar.

Leanna laughed. "Cora, you do remember we're in Winterspell, right? You make it sound like we're in an episode of *Love Island* or something."

I laughed and ordered a glass of wine when Gerry asked.

"I'm flying solo tonight. What about you?" she asked, tossing her thick spiral of curls off her shoulder. "I figured you'd be out with Clint."

I took a deep breath and shrugged out of my jacket, placing it on the back of my chair. "I just had dinner with him."

Leanna glanced at her watch. "Short and sweet, I guess?"

"Maybe not the sweet part." I couldn't help but frown.

Leanna cast me a sympathetic smile. "Gerry, I think we're going to need you to leave the bottle out," she called to the large barkeep as he poured my glass.

"Of course," he said, his accent thick, as he placed both the glass and the bottle in front of me.

"Thanks, Gerry."

The Scotsman nodded, then turned away to tend to his other patrons.

Leanna adjusted herself on the stool, twisting toward me. "So, do you want me to be your relationship therapist tonight or are we just going to drink until we forget our woes?"

I laughed. "I'm not sure yet."

"We'll start with a drink and see how things go."

Silently, I raised my glass in a toast.

I was in good company. Leanna never failed to cheer me up, no matter how gloomy I felt. Somehow, she could always snap me out of a sullen mood. She took a sip from the black straw in her drink, then stirred it around the remnants and frowned. "I'm going to need another myself, soon."

"A free one?" I teased.

Leanna flashed a wide grin as she held up her fingers and crossed them. "*Girl*, that is the hope."

"Any prospects so far?" I asked, taking a peek around the bar.

"Not as promising as I'd hoped." Leanna shrugged. "One guy came over, trying to start something up, but he reeked of cigarettes. I had to make up an excuse to slip off to the ladies' room. When I got back, he'd moved on."

"Small mercies," I said.

"So, you wanna talk about tonight?"

I shrugged and glanced at the burgundy liquid inside my wineglass. Leanna already knew most of the details about the deal Clint had with his mother because she'd been the first person I'd told. We never kept secrets from each other.

"Things are just tense," I said with an exhale. "I told him I wouldn't marry for money, regardless of how much I care about him. He asked if I would consider moving to Chicago, for him, and I told him I couldn't do that. Neither of us wants to try long distance. So … I guess we're kind of at an impasse, and I'm not sure where we go from here."

Leanna frowned. "What do you *want* to do?"

I smiled. "Rewind time, back to before that terrible dinner."

Leanna's smile was empathetic. "If I find a time machine, you'll be my first call. But until then…"

"I know." I bobbed my head. "I need to make a decision one way or the other. Dragging it out just means we'll have more of these awkward, tense dates."

"Agreed." Leanna caught Gerry's attention and raised her glass, indicating she was ready for a refill. He quickly swiped away the empty and she continued.

"Listen, Cora, you know I like Clint. I think you two make for a really great couple."

I winced. "I feel a *but* coming on."

"*But*," Leanna said with a smile, "I think long-term relationships require a lot of work to maintain. Yours is still new, so if it's this hard and complicated already, I'm not sure what that means for the future."

She paused and studied me for a reaction.

My shoulders drooped a couple inches, along with my sagging heart. "I know what you mean. It's what I've been thinking, too, if I'm honest. Clint is so different from anyone I've dated before. Which may have been part of what drew me to him, but now those differences are causing issues. I never wanted some fancy life, living in a big city."

I paused to sip at my wine, my mind flashing through images of what I imagined that would look like. He'd described bits of it before. A condo in a high-rise building, spending most nights out on the town, all glitzy and glammed up, wining and dining clients and potential clients. If I lived there with him, I'd be expected to tag along. The weekends would be spent at exclusive charity events or vacationing at luxury resorts where even more networking could be done.

For some people, that would be a dream life. But for me, it sounded like a nightmare.

"It just doesn't make sense," I added, shaking my head slightly as I set my glass down. "He was really enjoying Winterspell. He told me so a dozen times. He said he liked the slower pace and how friendly everyone is. He said he could see himself here, long term."

Leanna nodded. "Well, it sounds like that may be true, but he'd need his mother's money, right?"

"I guess." My chest tightened again, almost like my heart was bracing for the impact. "I can't marry him just so he can get it, though, Lee. I'd always wonder in the back of my mind whether our marriage was … real."

"That's fair."

"As much as you probably don't want to hear this, I'm going to say it anyway. Sometimes relationships fizzle out. People drift apart, have different interests, and their lives branch off in different directions. When that happens, it's not usually anyone's fault." She paused and took a reflective sip of her drink, pinching the straw between her thumb and index finger. "It's just one of those things that happens."

"You're right." I smiled. "That's not what I wanted to hear."

I took another sip of wine while Leanna laughed softly. "I'm just *saying* that maybe it's a blessing in disguise that you guys are stalling out right now. Take the time for self-care and to analyze what you want. Make a pros and cons list."

"You and your pros and cons lists," I teased.

"Hey now," Leanna shrugged. "They work."

"They do," I agreed.

Leanna bumped her shoulder against mine and cut me a playful smile. "If you *do* decide to call it quits with Clint, I wouldn't mind having my wing-woman back."

I laughed and tucked a strand of hair behind my ear. "Is that what you think I am?"

"We're like Thelma and Louise," she said.

"Which one am I?"

Leanna's lips quirked to one side for a moment. Then she replied, "Thelma."

"Drats. I wanted to be Louise."

We both laughed.

"At any rate, the single ladies train would love to have you back."

"Thanks," I laughed. "For putting that song in my head."

Leanna jumped down from her stool. "I know just what we need to put on the jukebox!"

She wandered across the bar, humming Beyoncé's hit song to herself. Moments later, Single Ladies (Put a Ring on It) was piping through the speakers, leading to an uproar from the other ladies around the bar. Leanna beckoned me to join her out on the makeshift dance floor. I shook my head, but Leanna's puppy-dog eyes worked their magic and pulled me away from the security of my barstool before the second verse.

At least Selene wasn't there to witness any of my dance moves.

10

The following morning, I sent a text message to Tabitha before heading to Wicked Wicks. Lily was scheduled to have the day off, and while I knew she would come in if I asked, I didn't want to take advantage of her kindness. Selene slipped out of the shop sometime before lunch and didn't return until it was close to closing time.

Despite her multitude of requests-slash-demands, I hadn't yet installed a cat flap at Wicked Wicks. Mostly because adding one to the kitchen door at home had been a pain in the rear. She appeared at the front door and tapped the glass impatiently with one paw, continuing the *tap tap tap* even after she could see me heading in her direction.

Frowning, I pulled open the front door. "Where have you been all day?"

She went straight to the counter and jumped up,

then leaped to her normal cubby near the front window. "Out," she replied.

Muttering to myself, I let the door swing closed and went back to the display I'd been working on. Somehow, even among the search for Aunt Lavender, I'd managed to create a new line of candles. They were inspired by a custom order and enchanted to display various scenes set at a carnival. There was one that made the room look like the inside of a carousel, complete with painted horses and shimmering gold lights—minus the dizzying effect of spinning round and round. Another smelled like kettle corn and had stalls of various carnival games. The third one smelled like cotton candy and featured silly clowns. I'd made sure to put a warning label on them. One witch's dream was another witch's night terror, after all.

Selene was critical of the idea—and she *really* didn't like the testing process I'd gone through to find the exact right scents—but I'd already sold four of the new sets.

"Be cagey if you want," I told the sourpuss. "It doesn't bother me. I have enough on my mind."

"Oh, so you're too busy to talk about what I found in Sal's records, then?"

My hand stilled, my fingers wrapped around a tall pillar candle. I peeked around the end of the display, to her glowing eyes. She flicked her tail. Clearly amused.

I sighed. We both knew I would take the bait.

"What are you talking about?"

"We didn't get to see everything the other day. Not with Lurch hanging around, all moon-eyed over Tabitha."

"You noticed that too?"

"Um, duh, Cora. I have eyes." She scoffed. "Anyway, I went over there to take another look around."

My eyes narrowed. "Do I even want to ask how you got inside?"

She puffed out her chest. "I slipped into a window I magicked open the day before."

"Selene…"

"What?"

"You shouldn't have done that. We have Ernesto's trust right now. We don't want to change that. We can't go over there without permission."

"You're being paranoid. No one was even there to see me. And what the oaf doesn't know won't hurt him."

I finished arranging the candles, then joined her at the front counter. "I'm just trying to be careful."

"Careful isn't going to find Lavender," Selene replied, her tone a little sharper than normal.

"Oh, come on," I said. "Don't be like that."

Selene licked her paw before responding. I knew she was doing it on purpose. She loved to keep me in suspense whenever she was annoyed with me.

"You know how much I want to find Aunt Lavender," I added. "What did you find? Anything we can use?"

Selene eyed me for another long moment, then lowered her paw. "I found out who installed the secret vault."

"Who?"

"It was James Midnight."

"Huh. I guess that makes sense though." I leaned against the counter. "He has that workshop."

"We should go and talk to him," Selene said.

I blinked. "You can't possibly think that James Midnight had anything to do with this."

"You never know about people."

I frowned at her. "I know that James Midnight is a well-respected citizen. His mother-in-law was one of the town's founding members, for the goddess's sake!"

"I'm not saying he's a suspect," Selene scoffed. "But he *would* know how the vault worked. For all we know there might be some magical tracking spell built into it. Or he could tell us whether or not someone could detect the magic used to conceal the room."

"I don't know." I glanced out the window and frowned. "It seems like a bit of a stretch."

"It can't hurt to speak to the man, Cora. What else are we going to do? Where's Tabitha?"

"I honestly don't know. I texted her this morning, letting her know where we would be, and I haven't heard from her all day. I hate to say it, but maybe she's given up on us."

"Hmm. I find that hard to believe. We'll go look for her after we talk to James." Selene gave a nod, indicating she'd made her executive decision on the matter. "Oh, and since we'll be passing it by, let's stop at the fish market on our way. I'm running low on tuna steaks."

A laugh helped release some of my tension and I smiled. "How convenient for you to mention dinner. That's been your motive all along."

"What?" Selene feigned innocence. "We have to eat, don't we?"

I rolled my eyes and grinned at her.

"We'll see how the meeting goes. Don't worry. You'll get your precious dinner."

"WHAT ARE WE SUPPOSED TO SAY?" I asked, flicking a glance in the rearview mirror as I slowed to a stop at a four-way intersection.

"Lie," Selene said from her usual place in the passenger seat. "Tell him you're renovating your house and want to explore your options for adding some magical storage. He doesn't know you live in a tiny shack and have zero money."

I shot the cat a scowl as I rolled through the intersection.

Selene wasn't finished. With a flourish of her tail, she continued. "Tell him you want to add a wing for yours truly, and that I demand the highest levels of security for my feline fortress!"

"Right." I rolled my eyes.

The Midnight family lived in a farmhouse that sat on a large piece of property just across the street from the waterfront. The home was well-maintained but had a lived-in look to it. A metal outbuilding stood a few paces from the home's wraparound porch and served as both the home's garage and the workshop where James and his mother-in-law, Rose, worked on their magical inventions.

The business wasn't technically open to the public, but it was listed in the Winterspell White Pages, so I didn't think it would raise any flags, us showing up uninvited. Even still, a nervous sensation pricked in my stomach as I parked my car in the driveway behind an old work truck.

The garage doors were all closed up, so Selene and I went to the door on the side and knocked. James Midnight answered the door, his dark hair slightly disheveled as though he'd been dragging his fingers through it.

"Hello," he said, giving both me and Selene a quick once-over. "Can I help you?"

"Hello, Mr. Midnight. My name is Cora Hearth, and this is Selene." I gestured at the cat. "I run Wicked Wicks, the candle shop here in town."

"Oh, of course." His hazel eyes lit up with recognition. "I saw your speech at the town hall meeting not too long ago. My wife, Penelope, has been to your shop a few times since."

My cheeks warmed and I ducked my chin. "Oh, thank you. That's very kind."

"Come inside," James said, stepping back to allow us entrance. He carried himself well, his build lanky but agile. He had to be somewhere in his fifties or sixties, considering the age of his grown daughters. His long, lean face curved into a welcoming smile. His strong nose jutted out past an angular chin. His thick brows were unruly above his eyes, wooly like caterpillars and fluctuating with each facial expression he made.

We followed him into the shop. It smelled like a combination of metal, wood, and something that could only be described as magic. A large yellow dog came over to greet us, and Selene recoiled. "Ugh! Get your hot breath out of my face; I know where your tongue has likely been. Filthy beast."

"Selene!" I hissed, nudging her rear with the toe of my boot.

James chuckled and snapped his fingers to get the pooch's attention. "Samantha, go to bed," he said.

The dog looked at him, then trotted over and collapsed with a *huff* on a buffalo-plaid dog bed near the woodstove.

"Sorry about her," I told James, still frowning at my difficult companion.

James smiled and slid his hands into his pockets. "It's not a problem. None of our cats talk—well, other than to Rosella, my oldest daughter. Have you two met?"

I shook my head. "I think I was a few years ahead of her in school."

"Oh, so you're from Winterspell?"

"All my life," I said with a smile.

"Believe me, she doesn't get out much," Selene scoffed.

The workshop was warm and cozy, if not a bit chaotic. The walls were covered in pegboard, allowing for a plethora of tools and gadgets to be displayed and at the ready. Large tables dominated most of the floor space, each showing a different project. James was known for taking nonmagical items and adding enchantments to them, to improve their functionality. My mom had one of his popular calendars that was something like a magical version of a Google calendar. A lot of people in Winterspell were technology resistant, preferring to use magic even when modern devices performed the same function. Granted, with something from James's workshop there were no viruses or glitches or power cords to worry about.

The door opened behind me, and I turned just as Rose Winters came into the shop, her nose buried in a battered paperback that featured a bare-chested pirate on the front. She nearly barreled into me, and I hurried to step out of her path.

"Um, Rose," James said, clearing his throat. "We have a customer."

Rose glanced up over the page and blinked at me. "Oh! Well, don't mind me, dear." She veered off and took a seat on a stool by the back wall.

James shook his head, his expression a mix of amused bewilderment. "Please, tell me, how can I help you? Did you need something designed for your shop?"

"Actually, I was hoping that you could answer a few questions for me."

James cocked his head to the side and gave me a curious glance. "Oh?"

"Well," I began, shifting my weight. "It's about that vault you made for Salvatore Greco."

If he was surprised, he hid it well. His brows barely twitched as he inclined his head. "I see."

"The one in his library," I added. "His, uh, nephew, Ernesto, told us you made it for his uncle. Is that true?"

I didn't look down at Selene. I knew she'd be grinning like an idiot, gleeful that I'd taken her suggestion to outright lie to the man.

"Yes, I made that," James replied with a nod. "It was some time ago. I've done a few secret rooms around town. They're quite intense projects, though."

"I can imagine. I'm not sure I even understand how it works. To have a room formed where there logically isn't space for one. It defies physics."

James smiled. "Doesn't most magic?"

I returned his polite smile. "I suppose that's true."

"What would you like to know about the vault?"

"Obviously, it's well hidden. But are there any security measures built in? Any additional magic meant to keep Sal's rarest books safe?"

"Oh, yes. Salvatore was most specific. He wanted the vault spelled to the books themselves. It was an extremely complicated piece of magic work, unlike anything I've ever done before."

"*We've* ever done before," Rose chimed in from her perch, not so much as taking her eyes off her book.

James smiled. "Right."

"How does it work?"

"Essentially, there is a spell Salvatore could cast on each book as it was taken into the vault. After the book was bound to the vault, it was impossible to remove. If someone tried to leave with one of those books, it would become so heavy it would be like trying to drag a two-ton anchor. I offered to put magical wards on the vault instead, but he was adamant that the books themselves be bound by the magic. He said they were too important. He worried that wards could be tampered with or broken."

"Salvatore, you clever old goat," Selene said, seemingly to herself.

"I did add a security alarm," James said. "In case someone tried to remove a book. Not only would the book itself be too heavy to lift, but a silent alarm would sound in Salvatore's mind, as a backup precaution."

"I guess that's why he didn't mind opening his library to researchers and university students," I said.

"He knew his most valuable collection was safe and sound."

James nodded. "That was the goal."

"Is there any way to know if anyone triggered that alarm in the last few months?"

"Only Sal would have that information," James answered, a touch of sadness in his eyes. "He was a good man. Taken far too soon."

Selene and I exchanged a glance with each other before looking at James.

"Well," I said after a lapse in the conversation. "Thank you for your time. I know you're a busy man, so, thanks for shaving off a little sliver of it to talk to us."

"It's no problem at all," James replied, kindness in his eyes as he escorted us to the door. "I'm sorry I couldn't be of more help."

We'd heard those exact same words so many times since beginning the search for Aunt Lavender. Round and round we went, only to end up at the end of another dead-end road.

$\mathcal{W}$e headed home after our brief meeting with James, our spirits lower than before. Tabitha still hadn't called or returned my text message. I was halfway tempted to stop by her hotel and see if she'd checked out and left town altogether. Instead, we went to the fish market right before closing and cleaned out their stock of tuna steaks.

"I swear, I'm about to trade this thing in for a pickup truck, so we can load your stinky cuisine in the back and leave my upholstery out of it," I grumbled to the cat as we drove away from the market.

Selene flashed her canines, her eyes sparkling. "Just make sure you get a step stool to cart along with you. Even with running boards I think you'd make a spectacle of yourself every time you tried to get in the driver's seat."

"You're *so* hilarious, Selene. We should get you a gig at Merlin's Well on stand-up night."

She began humming "The Lollipop Guild," her tail twitching in time with the chorus.

My jaw clenched. I was going to burn her tuna black.

While I was busy dreaming up ways to torment the furry feline, my phone rang in the cupholder. We were nearly home, so I reached over and picked it up.

"Someone's gonna get a ticket!" Selene cheered.

"It's Mom," I told her, tapping the accept call button. "Hey, Mom. What's up?"

"Cora, where are you?" Her voice trembled, the fear palpable in her tone.

A cold chill ran down my spine. "Mom? What's wrong?"

"I need you to come over. It—it's about Lavender."

I gripped the steering wheel and tossed a wary glance at Selene. The cat's amusement was gone, her ears now on alert as she listened to my side of the phone call.

"What happened?" I asked, my pulse thundering in my ears as I pulled into a driveway and turned my car around.

"I can't explain it over the phone." Mom's voice rose another octave. "Just come quick."

"I'm on my way."

I hung up so I could focus on the road. Winterspell wasn't a huge town, but there were several stop signs and red lights on the way from one side to the other. My mind raced, churning out half a dozen worst-case scenarios as I whipped across town, flying through intersections just as the lights switched from green to yellow.

"We're not going to get there at all if you keep driving like this!" Selene shouted, her front paws on the dashboard as she tried to anchor herself.

"I know what I'm doing." I stared through the windshield, my jaw tight, my voice firm.

"I don't want to die in a fiery car crash," Selene hissed.

"You're invincible, remember?"

I pushed the pedal harder with my foot to make it through another yellow light.

"Mee—oewww!" Selene shrieked.

Despite Selene's complaining, we made it to Mom's house intact. Both Selene and I launched out of the car as soon as I cut the engine.

Selene yelled at me over one shoulder as she bounded ahead, up the front steps. "I'm giving this Uber driver one star!"

"Fine by me," I snapped. "I won't have to cart you, or your fishy feast, all over town anymore."

Mom threw open the front door, cutting off the rest of our argument. Her hands were shaking. Her eyes were wide, her face pale as if she'd just witnessed a horrible crime. Her bottom lip trembled, and her red-rimmed eyes were glossy with tears.

I wrapped my arms around her, clutching her trembling frame. "Mom, what happened? What's wrong?"

She pulled away, her chin down, her eyes fixed on her socked feet.

"It was awful," she murmured.

My stomach coiled into a knot.

"You said something about Aunt Lavender," I prompted, keeping my voice gentle and as calm as I could, all things considered. My hands cupped hers to keep them from shaking. "Tell me what happened."

"I did another divination, trying to reach Lavender again."

"Okay." I took a deep breath. "What went wrong?"

Mom licked her lips. She tried to focus on me with glassy eyes, but her gaze drifted past my shoulder, as if she were seeing into another realm. "I heard another snippet of conversation."

"Was it like the last time we tried?"

She nodded slowly, her chin quivering.

"What did you hear?"

I braced myself. I almost didn't want to know.

"I heard a man's voice," Mom squeaked. "The same man we heard before. He was asking questions about a book this time. He wanted to know where it was and if she tore out the pages."

My stomach cinched even tighter. A gasp clawed at my throat, but I forced it down. I had to remain calm, for my mother's sake. "Was there anything else?"

Mom lifted her eyes to me, her expression heart-breaking. "I heard Lavender's voice, too."

My throat constricted. "What did she say?"

Mom's eyes fluttered closed for a long moment. Another tear squeezed free and coursed down her cheek. "She sounded so afraid."

I pulled her into another embrace. "Oh, Mom. I'm so sorry. You should have called us sooner. We would have come to help."

Mom nodded against my head, then pulled back again. She swiped at her cheeks, even as more tears fell. "She kept insisting that she didn't know anything about the missing pages and that she had nothing to do with it. Her voice was so weak."

She gave me a pleading look. "Cora—do you think that's what Lavender was talking about the last time we heard her? When she was muttering about not letting someone find it, the goddess forbidding it, and all that? Something to do with this book?"

I knew I had to come clean. I cut a glance at Selene who sat at my ankles and peered up at me with an expectant gaze.

With a heavy exhale, I took Mom's hands. "There's something we need to tell you."

"What is it?" My mom was already horrified enough. Now I was going to drop a bomb and shatter her the rest of the way. But I couldn't wait any longer. She needed to know the full truth.

"We found the fragment of the Golden Lotus."

Mom's features froze with shock. "You—you're kidding. You must be." She stared at me with sheer disbelief.

"I'm not. Aunt Lavender had it well hidden. Between Odin's Odyssey and now this ... well, we think it's the reason behind her abduction. We're working with Tabitha—or, at least, we *were*—"

Mom's expression crumpled. "What do you mean *were*? Where's Tabitha gone?"

"I'm not sure." I reached up and rubbed my temple. A steady pulsing reverberated against my fingertips. "We didn't tell her that Lavender has the piece of the Golden Lotus, but she does know about the book."

"But what about these missing pages?"

"We're trying to figure that out right now."

My mom's eyes searched between us. "Did you already tell Tabitha about this?"

"No." I shook my head vigorously. "As much as we like Tabitha, we thought it best to keep that detail to ourselves."

"Good." Mom sighed with relief. "Keeping it a secret is probably the best bet. A secret like that—well, it's huge. I can't believe Lavender would keep something like that from me, her only sister."

Selene scoffed. "How do you think I feel?"

"At least we know she's still alive," I said, cringing a little at how it came out. "Do you have any idea why she can't seem to break through and speak directly *to* you through the divination link?"

Mom's gaze fell back to her feet. "I can't make heads or tails of it. If I had to guess, I'd say it has something to do with the magic holding Lavender captive. Whoever took her must know how powerful she is and could have her under some kind of magic-blocking spell. My magic can get close, but it can't touch hers."

I nodded slowly. It made sense, or at least, as much sense as it could to me. I was an air witch and used illusion spells without so much as thinking about it when I was crafting my candles, but my mother's magic was foreign to me.

"Mom, promise me you won't try a divination again without us here with you."

"I promise," she agreed without hesitation.

"We just need to hold on a little longer. I'm going to find whoever did this. I'm going to bring her back."

"Excuse me," Selene interjected, her ears pinned back flat against her head. "Since when are you flying solo?"

I couldn't help but smile at the grumpy cat's expression. "Sorry. *We* are going to bring her back. All of us."

Mom was still shaken, but after another embrace, she began to rally. Her tears stopped and she wiped her cheeks free of any lingering trace. With a sniffle, she headed inside the house, gesturing for us to follow her. "Come on. It's chilly out here. Do you think you could stay for dinner? I could use the company."

I hooked a thumb over my shoulder, gesturing back at my car. "Only if you're in the mood for tuna and have room in the freezer to keep the extra from thawing out in my front seat."

Selene perked up and sauntered inside. "Be sure to use some of that seasoning I like, Lilac. You know, the one with the little bits of dried citrus peel."

I rolled my eyes toward the overhang covering the porch. "Are we sure this isn't all some elaborate ruse that Aunt Lavender put on sheerly to get away from *her*?"

Mom and I exchanged a look, before she cracked a smile and followed Selene inside.

12

We stayed with Mom for several hours, only leaving once she'd fully recovered. I had to threaten to toss Selene over my shoulder and carry her out to the car like a sack of potatoes before the cat would stir from her place beside the fire. She'd eaten her weight in tuna at dinner and looked more like a fur-covered volleyball than a cat by the time she called it quits. She bellyached about it all the way home, complaining about her stomach every time I hit a pothole or minor bump in the road.

"You think you can make it inside on your own? Or shall I go next door and see if Mrs. Parker will let me use her stroller?" I asked before climbing out of the car.

The cat groaned as she got to her feet and attempted to stretch. "I'm coming, I'm coming. Yeesh, you sure are impatient. It's not like you have a hot date waiting inside."

I slammed the driver's door and stalked up the front walk. Selene used a burst of magic to open her door, then lumbered out and followed after me. I switched on the lights and set my purse and keys on the table beside the door.

Selene heaved herself up onto the couch and exhaled as she rolled to one side. I shrugged out of my coat and closed the front door. "What a day."

"I'm beginning to think you're right about Tabitha," Selene said.

My ears perked. "Run that by me one more time. I was *what,* now?"

The cat shot me an irritated glance. "You were right. Tabitha doesn't seem to want to help."

I stared off into space and nodded. "I wonder what happened. Was it something you said?"

"Hey!" the cat hissed. "Why would it be something I said? What about you?"

I chuckled. "You can't seriously be asking me that. You're a walking insult machine."

"Not to Tabitha! I actually respect her. Plus, she wants me to be a guest on her podcast."

Frowning, I ignored the cat and went to the kitchen for a can of sparkling water. I had a bottle of wine on the counter, but it would only make me sleepier. Despite the busy day, I needed to put in a couple more hours of brainstorming our next move before I could go to bed. There was a ticking clock in my head that refused to let me sleep just yet.

I trudged to my living room, trying to stir up the energy to call Tabitha. Exhaustion tugged at me, but I grabbed my phone and a notepad before plopping down at the opposite end of the couch from where Selene wallowed.

I drew my legs onto the couch and tucked a throw blanket around them before dialing Tabitha's number. I put the phone on speaker so Selene could listen in.

To my surprise, Tabitha answered on the second ring. "Hello?"

I blinked. "Tabitha? Hey, it's Cora and Selene."

"I'm sorry I haven't gotten back to you today," she said. "I had a few things crop up, and I figured you were busy at the shop."

A quiver of irritation prickled at me, but I shoved it aside with a mental reminder that she was helping us for free and also had a life outside the search for Aunt Lavender.

"Right. Well, actually I do have some news. Are you free to talk?"

"I'm working on a podcast episode," she said, "so I won't be able to meet up tonight."

I frowned. "Oh, okay."

"But I have a few minutes now," she added. "What's going on? Is everything okay?"

I proceeded to catch her up on the events of the day, starting with the information we'd received from James Midnight and then about the unsettling divination attempt.

"The good news is Lavender is alive," Tabitha said at my conclusion.

I nodded.

"And we know we are on the right track, with regards to the missing pages. Your gut instinct was right, Cora. Whoever took her is after the Odyssey. Remind me, where do you store it?"

"Oh, it's—"

Selene sunk a claw into my ankle.

"Ouch!" I exclaimed.

"What is it? Are you okay?" Tabitha asked, her voice alarmed.

I glared at the cat. Selene shook her head.

Still frowning, I shifted gears. "Oh, I'm fine. Just, uh, stubbed my toe is all."

"I hate that," Tabitha said, a touch of humor in her voice. "I always say I should wear my composite-toe boots everywhere. I'm a total klutz."

Somehow, I doubted that.

"The book is safe," I said. "No one will be able to find it."

There was a beat of silence, and I almost thought she was about to push for more information. A strange sensation swirled through my stomach as I looked over at Selene.

"Right, of course." Tabitha laughed it off. "I can meet you tomorrow when you're free. We can pick things up and hopefully find a new lead."

Selene nodded, her eyes intent on the phone.

I bobbed my head, too. "Yeah, absolutely. That sounds great to me."

We said goodbye and I hung up. "Okay," I said, rubbing at my ankle where Selene had struck. "You want to tell me what that was all about? You broke the skin!"

"Something isn't sitting right with me," Selene replied. "She goes MIA all day, and then when you get her on the phone, the thing she's most interested in is finding out where we keep the book. That doesn't seem at all fishy to you?"

"The only thing fishy is your breath," I grumbled, still inspecting my wound. "Tabitha is trying to help us. And by the way, contacting her in the first place was your idea!"

"What if she's just using us, though? For all we know, she's just here mining content for her next book deal or podcast series."

"I don't know where all the cynicism is coming from, but I think you're being ridiculous." I tossed the blanket back over my feet. For all my complaining, the scratch wasn't bleeding, so I wasn't worried about staining the fabric. "She's got a life. She dropped everything to come and help us, we should have expected she'd have other things to do and that she wouldn't be at our beck and call twenty-four seven."

Selene's whiskers twitched. "Fine, but we need to

watch what we say to her. Obin's Odyssey is valuable. We should be more careful with it."

"Technically, we should give it back to Ernesto. It never belonged to Aunt Lavender in the first place."

Selene's eyes narrowed. "What's he going to do with it?"

I shrugged one shoulder. "It's none of our business. It belongs to Sal's estate, which is now his to do with as he pleases."

Selene stretched out on the couch, her stomach still more rounded than usual. "You know, you could sell it off yourself, use the money to entice your little Clinty-poo to stay in town."

The remark hit the center of my chest. "Why don't you stay out of it? Okay. I shouldn't have even told you. I should have known you'd hold it over my head or use it to insult me."

"Oh, come on, Cora. Don't be like that. I'm just teasing."

I tapped the screen of my phone. I'd been checking it all day, in hopes of hearing from Tabitha. But there was another notable absence among my notifications.

With a sigh, I tossed the phone and notepad to one side and pushed off the couch. The bottle of wine was calling my name, and I was too tired to resist.

I was no closer to finding a solution to the Clint problem than I was to finding Aunt Lavender. It wouldn't do me any good to sit awake all night, banging my head against the same ideas.

Relief, at least for the moment, would only be found at the bottom of a glass of merlot, and then in the comfort of my own bed.

13

*W*hen the bell on the front door rang the following morning, I was wrist deep in wax and wicks, hunched over a bowl as I worked on a batch of charisma-boosting candles, meant to be burned prior to an important job interview, presentation, or simply to banish the first-date butterflies. The effect of the magic was even working on me, largely reducing the doom and gloom left lingering after the night before.

"I'll be right with you!" I called out from the back room, craning my neck for a partial view of the register. Lily wasn't in yet, but she always used the back entrance.

I was wiping my hands clean when I heard a customer exclaim, "Oh my stars! It's Tabitha Hardwick!"

"Well, well," Selene purred from her perch, "look who decided to show up."

"Shh!" I scowled at the cat and tossed the towel aside. Plastering a smile in place, I stepped out into the front of the shop. "Good morning, Tabitha."

She stood near the door wearing her signature black, calf-high boots, paired with an eggplant-colored wrap dress. Her tresses were tied up into a high bun, in a way that looked effortless, almost to the point of looking sloppy, but had likely taken twenty minutes to create.

It made me grateful for my easy-breezy, short-cropped locks.

Tabitha tossed me a smile, but her attention was quickly pulled away as half a dozen customers circled around her, asking for autographs and selfies.

"Can I get your autograph?" Matilda, one of my regulars, asked.

Tabitha flashed her famous grin. "I would love to if I had anything to write—"

Without hesitation, Matilda waved her fingers in front of her purse, and it popped opened, shooting out both a notepad and pen in a geyser of pink sparkles.

"Oh my!" Tabitha exclaimed. "That's quite the party trick."

Matilda offered a sheepish smile. "I have a tendency to lose things, so my essentials are spelled to be easily found."

"Quite clever," Tabitha replied, taking the pen and

pad. She scribbled her name and handed both back to the witch with a grateful nod.

As soon as she finished, another woman stepped forward. "I just *love* your podcast. I don't miss a single episode."

Tabitha smiled and took the woman's pen and paper. "That's very sweet," she said as she signed the page.

"I've listened to them all at least three times," the woman said loudly, as though bragging to the others in the small crowd. "Whenever I get to the last episode, I just start all over again. My husband thinks I'm nuts!"

Tabitha laughed politely and handed back the pen and paper. "That's the highest compliment. Thank you."

"Give me a *break*," Selene muttered.

I slid a glance toward the cat. "I remember your face when I told you Tabitha emailed us back. So … I'm not sure you really have room to talk."

Selene's tail thumped the counter.

Tabitha signed autographs left and right, answering questions and taking photos on cell phones in between each one. The ruckus drew in random passersby, and after half an hour, my shop looked like it did at the peak of tourist season.

"What a zoo," Selene grumbled.

I shrugged. "At least it's drawing in business."

"Did you hear the new episode she dropped this morning? You know, the one that was *so* important she couldn't be bothered to help us all day."

I shook my head. "I haven't had a chance to listen."

Selene's ears went flat. "She interviewed some whack-a-do who has dedicated the last ten years of their life to traipsing through the Everglades, looking for river dragons. River dragons! Have you ever heard of anything so ridiculous? They're called crocodiles, and they're damn near everywhere down there!"

"Calm down, Selene. We can't expect her to drop everything for us. Like she said, it's all scheduled and contracted out."

I reverted my gaze to Tabitha who was still busy answering questions to fans and not paying attention to Selene's complaints, thank goodness.

"And don't talk so loud," I whispered. "She's standing right there."

"Can my daughter take a selfie with you?" A slender woman made her way to the front of the line, her hands clutching the shoulders of a shy little girl with shoulder-length, straight, honey-brown hair.

"Of course!" Tabitha exclaimed, immediately squatting down to get more eye level with her young fan.

It took some time, but eventually the crowd began to disperse. A few people lingered in the shop, some even made purchases, and when things cleared out, Tabitha approached the counter, a delighted grin on her face.

"It must be exhausting, being so popular," Selene muttered.

"Selene!" I hissed through clenched teeth, cutting

her a reprimanding look before turning my attention to Tabitha. "I'm sorry—"

Tabitha's smile was unflappable. She tossed her hand through the air, dismissing the comment. "It doesn't bother me a bit."

I gave her a wary smile. "It looks like you have quite the fan base."

"All part of the gig," she replied with a simple shrug. "It's kind of nice, the dichotomy of it all. I go for weeks, sometimes months, alone on some quest in the middle of nowhere. Then when I resurface and return to my normal life, I can't get a moment to myself. Usually by the time I start feeling too *peopled out*, it's time to hit the road again. So, it works."

"I heard your new episode," Selene told her, and I cringed at her sharp tone.

I shot her a glacial stare, which she ignored entirely.

Tabitha didn't seem to notice either way. She clapped her hands together and her smile grew wider. "Wasn't Martin a hoot? Oh, stars, I could have talked to him all day. Who knew there were dragons in Florida?"

"There aren't," Selene fired back. "The guy was a total crackpot. I'm starting to question the pedigree of your show. I'm not sure I want to be lumped in with Florida Man and the quest for magic gators."

"Selene, stop. You're being rude."

Tabitha's eyes narrowed slightly, the edges of her smile twitching, as she formed her reply. "I try to have a broad spectrum of guests on my show. Variety is the spice of life, as they say. But, hey, no hard feelings if you've changed your mind about doing an episode together."

I held up a hand and took a side step to block the snarky cat from Tabitha's view. "Let's all just take a step back from that. Um, so, I know you were busy with the show, but did you happen to come up with any ideas for the search? As I said on the phone last night, we ended up chasing our tails."

Tabitha flicked her gaze from the wall behind me, where Selene lay crouched in a cubby, and she drew in a quick breath. With a blink of her aqua eyes, she rearranged her smile and gave me an enthusiastic nod. "Yes, actually. I was stopping by to tell you that after we spoke, I got a chance to check my messages, and one of them was from a Golden Lotus scholar. Wilton Moses."

"A Golden Lotus *scholar*?" My eyebrows raised and so did my pulse. "I didn't realize that was even a thing. That would have been helpful three weeks ago."

"It's an unofficial title, of course. But Wilton has spent decades studying the legend of the Golden Lotus, and he gave me some juicy insight." She dug into the satchel hanging at her hip and produced a folded sheet of paper.

She handed it to me, and I opened it to reveal a printed email correspondence between Tabitha and Wilton.

"As you know, there are two pieces that make up the

Golden Lotus. They have to be together to make the spell work to reveal the Fountain of Youth."

I bobbed my head as my eyes skipped ahead, scanning the email conversation.

Tabitha continued. "Wilton says that the two pieces of the Lotus will actually *call out* to one another, so to speak. There's some kind of magical, magnetic pull between them if they get close enough."

"Really? How interesting."

Tabitha nodded. "Now, Wilton has actually seen Obin's Odyssey, and he said the pages that pertain to the Lotus were indeed intact when he last saw it, some seven or eight years ago. And according to him, there is an incantation in the book, and the lettering was made by ink infused with melted gold scrapings from the Lotus itself!"

I glanced up, my eyes widening.

Tabitha's eyes were alight with wonder. "So, I think it's possible that the Golden Lotus pieces would *call out* if they were close enough to the pages from the Odyssey!"

Selene made a scoffing sound.

My cheeks warmed. "Sorry, she probably has a hairball."

"I do *not*," Selene protested, jumping onto the front counter to once more insert herself into the middle of the conversation.

Tabitha gave the cat an expectant glance. "You don't think my theory is correct?"

"Maybe it is, maybe it isn't," Selene said with a casual flick of her tail. "But unless you've got a piece of the Lotus hidden inside that messy bun thing of yours, it isn't going to help us out much in our current situation."

"Selene, what has gotten into you?" I demanded. "Why are you being so rude?"

Before the feline could explain her foul mood—or, more likely, fire off another insult—the bell on the front door chimed once more. On autopilot, I slapped on a smile and turned to greet my customer, only to lock eyes with Bernadette Wise, Salvatore's maid.

She licked her lips as her gaze pinged between the three of us, then she clenched her hands together in front of her and said, "I need to speak with you. It's about that vault."

14

*B*ernadette shifted her weight, glancing over one shoulder to look through the glass on the door behind her. "I hope it's okay that I stopped by in the middle of the day like this."

I glanced at Tabitha; her confusion mirrored that in my own mind. "Of course it is. Why wouldn't it be?"

Bernadette turned back to face us. She reached up and tucked a tendril behind one ear and I realized her eyes were puffy, like she'd been crying or had had a particularly bad night's sleep. "I wasn't sure how to find you, so I asked Ernesto, and he said something about a candle shop. I figured this was the place," she said, her voice almost raspy.

I offered a polite smile, doing my best to keep my curiosity in check. The woman was clearly nervous. I didn't need to do anything to spook her before she could tell me what she wanted to say.

There were a few customers in the shop, mostly minding their own business, poking around the shelves and displays. Lily was still absent, though her shift wasn't set to start for another thirty minutes. Most days she arrived early, but something must have come up.

"Is there somewhere we can talk in private?" Bernadette asked, her attention zeroing in on me.

"Of course." I looked at Selene. "Can you watch the front for a few minutes?"

The cat's eyes widened. "You can't be serious! What do you expect me to do? Charm the customers? Freshen up the displays? *Make change?*"

I squeezed my eyes closed for a moment. "You could just say *no.*"

"Okay, fine. No."

Bernadette reached behind her, one hand on the door. "I can come back later."

"No!" Tabitha and I both said, our voices amplifying as they combined.

A few customers looked over and my cheeks warmed. "Sorry about that," I said, making eye contact with those nearest the counter. "If you need anything, just let me know."

I was about to tell Tabitha to take Bernadette into the storeroom alone when I caught sight of Lily in my peripheral vision as she came down the sidewalk in front of the building. She wore a dreamy smile, singing along with whatever was playing through her white earbuds.

"Bernadette, this way," I said, gesturing her away from the door. "We can speak in my office, if you'll forgive my mess."

Bernadette gave me a small smile. "I'd be in the wrong line of work if a little mess frightened me off."

I laughed softly. "That's true."

Tabitha led the way and Bernadette followed. Lily swept into the shop, smiling at the customers with her signature sweetness. She stopped to straighten a stack of tea lights on her way to greet me at the register. "Morning, Cora! Isn't it so nice outside? I would have been here earlier, but I couldn't resist an extra-long walk with Peanut this morning."

"It is a good day for it. How is Peanut, anyway? Still not sleeping through the night?"

Lily had adopted a ten-week-old pit bull puppy from a shelter the weekend before—a cautionary tale of the consequences of just popping in to an adoption fair—and while the little chubby bundle couldn't have been cuter, he was also giving the first-time dog owner a bit of a run for her money.

Lily laughed as she pulled her purse off over her head. "Oh, he slept just fine. He had a busy night, eating the sole of one of my Converse sneakers while I made dinner. The new puppy playpen is being delivered tomorrow."

I winced before joining her lighthearted laughter. "Probably a good call. Where is he today?"

"Oh, my mom took him off my hands for the day. She's a saint." Lily came around the counter and stashed her jacket and purse in one of the cabinets. "So, how are things here?"

"Pretty steady," I replied. "Listen, I'll catch you up on a few things, but first, there's something I need to take care of in the back. Can you clock in a little early and hold down the fort?"

"Of course!"

"Thanks. You're the best!"

With Lily at the helm, I slipped into the storeroom and found Tabitha and Bernadette seated on a pair of shipping crates I hadn't gotten around to unpacking yet. Selene was perched on a high shelf, surveying the scene from above. Her ethereal blue eyes drifted my way, and she straightened her posture. "There you are. Let me guess, Lily was regaling you with stories of her precious little drool box?"

I rolled my eyes. "Peanut doesn't drool. He's just teething right now. It'll pass."

"Oh, right. The walking flea resort will wake up in a few weeks smelling of roses and spearmint. I'm sure."

Tabitha cleared her throat, gently drawing my attention back to the matter at hand.

"Sorry to keep you waiting," I told Bernadette. "Now, what is it you wanted to tell us? You said something about the vault?"

Bernadette's expression crumpled, and for a moment I thought she was about to hop down from the crate and go running out the back exit. She swallowed hard and then bobbed her head a few times. "I—I lied to you before."

"Lied to us?" Tabitha's eyes narrowed. "About what?"

The woman stared down at her folded hands. "I told you I didn't know anyone else who knew about the secret vault in the library, but the truth is, I do."

"Okay," I replied, keeping my tone gentle. "Who else knows about it?"

Bernadette lifted her gaze. Her eyes flickered with sincere apology. "His name is Mickey Chapin."

I frowned at Selene and then looked back to Bernadette. "That name doesn't sound familiar to me."

"We were ... *involved*. Um, romantically."

Tabitha nodded once. "So, he was your boyfriend?"

Tabitha's tone was calm and free of judgment, but Bernadette flinched as if she'd physically lashed out at her. "We were in a romantic relationship, yes."

"Well, who is he? Does he know Sal?" I asked.

Bernadette exhaled as her gaze drifted toward the ceiling. "Mickey was a grad student doing research at Salvatore's estate over the summer. I'd see him there when I was working. I thought he was really handsome, but far too young for me, but then ... well, one night, he and I left at the same time. It was pouring, and we were both waiting on the porch. I figured he was just waiting for a break in the rain, like me, but he told me later that he was standing there, trying to muster up the courage to ask me to dinner."

A wistful smile played at Bernadette's lips. "We fell in love and spent every free moment we could with each other."

Tabitha crossed one leg over the other, lacing her hands over her knee. "So, did you tell him about the vault? Or did Sal?"

"I—I did. It was late one night. I'd had too many glasses of wine. And Mickey was frustrated. Sal had been teasing him about some sort of book he knew Mickey needed for his research. He was trying to get Mickey to buy it, but Mickey didn't have the money. Anyway … I may have let it slip that Sal kept things like that in a secret place."

My brows peaked. "Do you know the name of the book he wanted?"

Bernadette sniffled and shook her head. "I don't know. Something Odyssey I think."

My heart jumped. Tabitha looked like a caged tiger, about to pounce on a rack of ribs.

"Obin's Odyssey?" I asked Bernadette.

"Maybe? I don't really know." She squeezed her eyes closed. "I'm sorry. My head is just all over the place. We —well, I, ended things with Mickey last night."

Selene's eyes took on a familiar glow. I knew that look. It was the one she got while watching a juicy episode of trashy reality TV. All she was missing was a big tub of popcorn.

"I—I'm sorry to hear that," I said, jumping in before Selene could offer up her own commentary. "Do you think that he might have tried to go into the vault? To get that book?"

After our conversation with James Midnight, I knew his odds of success were almost zero, but still, it didn't hurt to ask. There was a reason Bernadette had sought us out to spill the secret.

"If you had asked me a day or two ago, I would have said no," Bernadette answered, conviction strengthening her voice. "But that was before I knew who the real Mickey Chapin was! The Mickey I thought I knew wouldn't have stolen a book, but he also wouldn't have wound up in some trollop's bed after going to his brother's bachelor party, either!"

Selene's eyes sparkled like a disco ball.

Bernadette crossed her arms over her ample chest. "I knew it was risky. Dating a younger man. All of my friends warned me. They said I should date someone my own age." She tossed her head in disgust, even as fresh tears sprang to her dark eyes.

"I mean, the man is named after a cartoon mouse. What did you really expect?" Selene asked.

"Selene!"

The cat flicked her tail. "What? All I'm saying is that if you hang out with a clown, expect a full circus."

"What—what does that even mean?" I scoffed. "You know what, never mind."

"All men are pigs," Selene added. "Just ask Cora. Her

boyfriend is trying to get her to marry him so he can get his mommy's money stash."

"That's it!" I straightened and shot a blast of fierce wind magic at the back door. It burst open with a loud *bang* as the metal hit the side of the building. Selene recoiled, but not fast enough. I scooped her up in another swirl of wind and sent her furry hindquarters out into the alley. When I was sure she was clear of the door, I pulled my wrist in toward my stomach and conjured the wind in the opposite direction, slamming the door closed once more.

Tabitha gave me an impressed smile. "Now, be honest, how worried are you that she's going to shred your upholstery in retaliation?"

I smacked my hands together a few times, releasing the almost static buzz from the residual magic. "She can try, but I don't think she'll risk ticking off her personal chef and chauffeur."

Bernadette looked bewildered by the whole exchange, and I imagined she was questioning the decision to ever step foot in my store.

"Sorry about that," I said, smoothing my hands down the front of my apron. "And I'm sorry about things with Mickey."

She shrugged her shoulders before letting them slump forward again. "It is what it is. I learned my lesson." She glanced up at me, then at Tabitha. "I should have told you about this the other day. But I didn't

145

want you to think he had something to do with the theft."

"Theft?" Tabitha's gaze flew to mine. "We didn't say anything about a theft, did we?"

"I just assumed that's what this was about," Bernadette replied. "I figured you were helping Ernesto track down some missing items now that he's dealing with selling off his uncle's estate. Sal told me he kept rare books in that vault. You come around, asking who knew about it. I might not have a fancy college education, but I can put two and two together."

Tabitha nodded, her lips slightly curved. "Of course. Sorry we weren't more straightforward. We're just trying to keep this matter fairly quiet."

Bernadette hopped down from the crate and made her way to the back door. "I still don't think Mickey had anything to do with this, but if he did, I hope you nail his cheating behind."

And with that, she slipped out into the alley and disappeared.

IT TOOK every shred of willpower to keep from closing down the shop and running off to locate Mickey Chapin immediately after Bernadette's departure. But

Tabitha refused to budge until we had a solid plan, and plans take time.

Selene eventually came back to the shop—sulking over my so-called beastly behavior. Lily indulged the cat's grievances, while I tried not to roll my eyes so hard they fell out of my head.

"Now, now, you two," Lily said, giving Selene a pat on the head, "you just need to move past it. Even the best of friends have their moments."

Selene made a gagging noise. "You think *she* is my best friend?"

Lily's expression shifted, concern knitting between her fair brows. "She's your witch. You're her familiar."

"Ha! Not by choice," Selene scoffed.

"It's a long story," I told my bewildered associate. "Best not to get into it. Just leave Selene alone. She'll get over herself eventually."

Lily looked ready to protest, but a customer approached the counter, a different-colored candle in each hand, and asked her for advice. When she escorted the customer over to the appropriate shelf, I turned to Selene. "All right, furball, I'm sorry for tossing you out into the alley. I won't make excuses. I should have been more patient. However, in the future, please keep the details of my romantic life to yourself."

Selene looked away, her chin lifted ever so slightly.

I sighed. "Come on, Selene. We don't have time to be mad at each other. Once Tabitha finds out where

Mickey lives, we're going to confront him. We need to work together. For Aunt Lavender's sake."

"Fine!" She swished her tail a few times, still looking out the window. "But as soon as we find Lavender, we're going to find a spell that releases me from my duties."

My mouth dropped open. "You—you're serious?"

"Yes. It's clear this partnership has been a disaster from the start. We're incompatible, you and I."

"Selene … I said I was sorry—"

"It's fine, Cora." She finally shifted her attention back toward me, appraising me with cool eyes. "I'm not mad. I'm just tired."

I wanted to argue, to keep talking until she came around, but she jumped down from the counter and made her way to the front door. She timed her escape just right, slipping out in a customer's wake, thus avoiding having to ask for help getting the door open.

When she was gone, I tried to throw myself into work, but her absence weighed heavily on me for the rest of the day.

I never thought I would say it, but for once, I missed her.

$\mathcal{T}$abitha returned to the shop just before closing, armed with all of Mickey Chapin's information. Selene arrived not too long after, and I suspected she'd been watching the shop, waiting for Tabitha. We said goodnight to Lily and closed down the shop, waiting until the last of the customers had gone before launching into our planning.

"All right, so he lives in an apartment building just a few blocks from here," Tabitha said, tapping a nail against her notepad. "He's twenty-nine years old. He graduated a handful of years ago. I'm not sure what he's working on that would have led him to Sal's library in the first place, nor do I know his connection to Obin's Odyssey. It strikes me as interesting that Salvatore was dangling that in front of him. It must pertain to whatever he was working on. Right?"

I shrugged as I wiped down the front counter. I'd

worry about counting the till in the morning. My mind was far too busy to consider doing it now. "Maybe Sal was just bragging. It was a pretty rare find."

"Maybe." Tabitha tapped her nail again. "Anyway, I think we should just go talk to him. See what he knows. If what James said is true, there's no way he could have gotten his hands on the Odyssey even if he did know about the vault, but he probably spent a lot of time in Sal's library. He might have seen something. Overheard something."

"Worth a shot," I said, tossing the used paper towel. "I'm ready when you are."

Tabitha rode shotgun for the quick drive to the apartment building. It was technically close enough to walk, but we were all tired, and though the morning had started out pleasant, the afternoon had brought rain and thunder. I thought the weather was fitting, considering my dark mood. Selene still wasn't speaking to me, and the tension hung thick in the car as I drove to Mickey's.

Tabitha led the charge as we found the right building and climbed the steps to the third level. "This is the one," she said, stopping in front of unit 324. She adjusted the strap on her shoulder and brushed a loose strand of hair out of her eyes before cutting me a quick glance. "Ready?"

I released a long breath, wishing that my stomach would stop swirling. "Ready."

Tabitha knocked her fist against the door. Maybe it

was just the treasure hunter in her, or her familiarity with the public and comfort in the spotlight, but I basked in her confidence and wished I could steal a tiny slice of it for myself.

Somewhere nearby, a baby cried.

I straightened my posture when the door opened.

A man stood in front of us, a perplexed look on his face. His eyes were dark brown, his jawline strong, with a trace of stubble. A pair of glasses with thick black frames perched on the tip of his broad nose. He was handsome, as Bernadette had said, but not in a Hollywood sort of way. He was someone who might catch my eye if I saw him walk into a coffee shop, but not so devastating I would be too nervous to try and strike up a friendly chat.

He shoved one hand into the pocket of his dark blue jeans and arched a thick eyebrow. "Can I help you?"

"You're Mickey, right?" Tabitha asked. There was a familiarity to her tone, as though she were bumping into a friend of a friend on a trip to the market.

"That's me," he said, still mildly confused, though his interest in Tabitha was growing, judging by the slow once-over he gave her before answering. "Are you—"

"Tabitha Hardwick," she supplied, extending one hand toward him.

Mickey's other brow lifted, and he pumped Tabitha's hand. "I—I'm at a loss for words," he said, grinning at her. "I really enjoyed your book."

"Here we go again," Selene scoffed.

Mickey's attention snapped to the talking cat. "Oh?"

"Don't mind her," I said, offering my own hand. "My name is Cora and this is Selene. Do you have a few minutes to talk to us?"

Mickey reluctantly released his grip on Tabitha's hand to shake mine. When we finished, he raked his fingers through his dark hair, his gaze bouncing between Tabitha and me. "I'm sorry, but what is this about? I don't imagine this is a stop on some kind of PR tour," he said, flashing a charming smile.

"No," Tabitha replied, matching his casual grin. "However, I do think you might be of some help to me and my investigative work. A little bird told me that you were one of the students who frequented the late Salvatore Greco's personal library. Is that true?"

"That's right. One of my professors introduced me to Salvatore not too long before I graduated. I was still debating whether or not to go on to grad school, and Salvatore helped me make the decision. He offered his library to me whenever I was in Winterspell. At the time, I lived on the other side of the country."

Mickey paused and pushed his glasses up his nose. "After school, I took a teaching job here in Winterspell, and kept going to Salvatore's to do research for this book I'm writing."

"You're an author?" Tabitha asked. "We should get coffee sometime. Debate the Oxford comma over a pile of scones."

Mickey chuckled. "You name the time and place."

Tabitha placed a hand on my shoulder. "Now, Cora here, she knows Sal because he used to sell rare books to her aunt. Did you ever hear anything about that? Sal's book trade?"

Mickey's smile faltered and he quickly stuffed his hands into the front pockets of his jeans. "Um, rare book trade? No. I mean, wouldn't that be illegal, considering his position within the Order?"

Tabitha laughed, the sound light enough to be carried away on a gentle breeze. "Mickey, come on. This isn't some sting operation."

He glanced between us, unconvinced.

"Listen, I'll let you in on a little secret," Tabitha said, leaning in as she lowered her voice. "I'm looking for Obin's Odyssey, and word around the treasure hunter water cooler is that Sal might have gotten his hands on it shortly before he died. We spoke with his nephew, Ernesto, and he says the book was stolen."

Mickey rocked back on his heels. "You think so?"

Tabitha shrugged, as if she couldn't care less. "Makes sense. A book like that would fetch a pretty penny." She cast a glance above Mickey's head, focusing on the weather-worn siding of the apartment building, and the bulging gutter where a small plant had taken root, peeking over the side. "Enough money to get out of a town like Winterspell. That's for sure."

Mickey shook his head. "Well, I don't know

153

anything about it. Besides, Salvatore is gone now. He certainly wouldn't care where the book ended up."

"I'm not so sure," Tabitha replied. "Salvatore would have wanted his collection protected. Why else would he have gone through the trouble to have that secret vault installed? You do know about that, don't you?"

Mickey shrugged. "Maybe."

"But you don't know where Obin's tome might be?" Tabitha prompted. "No one would have to know. I have a buyer who would pay top dollar for it."

Mickey reached for the doorknob as he took a step backward. "I really don't know anything more. Good luck, though."

"Mickey—" Tabitha said.

But it was too late. He'd already gone back inside and closed the door. A moment later, the dead bolt clicked into place, leaving the three of us standing on the porch, dumbfounded.

"He definitely knows something," Selene insisted as we climbed back into my car. "He was wriggling like a worm on a hook!"

I nodded. "You did a really good job, Tabitha. He won't suspect Bernadette told us anything. I'd hate to make her life more complicated."

Tabitha shrugged off the praise. "We didn't need to bring her into it."

"Do you think he has the missing pages?" I asked her. My personal BS detector was blaring, but I couldn't fully trust my judgment. I was desperate for a lead, and I didn't want to steer us down another dead-end path just for the sake of doing something.

Tabitha exhaled, still staring at Mickey's apartment building. "I think he knows more than he's letting on, or he wouldn't have gotten all shifty, but I'm not convinced he's our guy."

Before I could form a new theory to test, Tabitha sat upright in her seat, her eyes narrowed. "Well now, where do you think you're going?"

I followed her gaze and spotted Mickey, now wearing a black coat, locking up his apartment. He jogged down the stairs and made his way to a silver sedan parked in the resident lot on the other side of the property from where we were parked.

When he swiveled in our direction to get behind the wheel, I instinctively ducked my chin.

"Follow him!" Tabitha exclaimed.

My fingers fumbled the keys and Selene growled in frustration as I bent to retrieve them. "I'm trying!" I huffed.

Tabitha gave directions and it didn't take long to catch up to Mickey. There was a car between us, but I didn't mind having the buffer. He didn't go far, only about four miles across town, to a cluster of homes in a mid-level neighborhood. He parked behind a red Civic in the driveway of a small blue house with white trim.

I drove past the house and parked a few houses down. As soon as I cut the engine, we all twisted around to see what was going on. A woman with long blonde hair and an hourglass figure came out to greet Mickey, all but pouncing him right there in the yard.

Not that Mickey seemed to mind. He roped his arms around the woman and the two leaned in to exchange a hot and heavy kiss.

"Ew," Selene spat. "Get a room."

"Pretty sure that's their plan," I said as the blonde took Mickey's hand and dragged him inside the house.

"Well, it looks like Bernadette was right about the side piece," Tabitha said with a heavy exhale. "Poor thing."

"Come on. There's nothing more to see here," I said, disappointed the whole encounter left us empty-handed.

"Well, there probably is," Selene quipped, "but we'd have to get closer to the windows."

Groaning, I put the car in drive and peeled away from the curb.

WE DROPPED Tabitha off at her hotel and picked up takeout from Whimzee's Deli. Selene liked their tuna salad, and I wasn't in the mood to cook. With Tabitha gone, the strained tension between Selene and me grew even more apparent. Normally, even when we were grumpy with each other, we'd talk. Selene would complain. I'd offer a counterargument. Round and round we'd go.

Tonight, it was silent.

I turned on the TV to provide a distraction—and maybe drudge up some conversation fodder—but it just wasn't the same. Selene kept her sharp commentary to herself and seeing the happy (for now) couples on *Love Island* was only making me miss Clint and the way things used to be.

How had my life fallen so completely apart in the space of a week?

Even my dinner wasn't sitting right with me.

Finally, I clicked the mute button and turned to Selene. "All right, what's it going to take to fix this?"

Selene was in the middle of her post-dinner bath, but she paused her grooming long enough to glance up at me, one paw hovering in the air. "There's nothing to fix, Cora." She exhaled and lowered her paw to the sofa cushion. "We both said some stupid things. Can we just move on?"

I frowned. "Is that your way of apologizing?"

"It's my way of saying shut your yap and turn the TV back on."

"Selene, this is more important than the stupid show. I'm really trying here."

"You want to make it up to me?"

Dread squeezed my heart. She was either going to ask for a full-time cat assistant, or maybe a deep freezer filled with halibut.

"I have an idea," she continued. "You won't like it, but I think it could get us some answers. You go along with the plan, and I'll let bygones be bygones."

I raised a brow. "What is the plan?"

Selene flicked her tail. "That Mickey guy was lying about something. I'd bet my robot litter box he knows about the book, and you know how much I love that thing."

"Okay…"

"I say we test Ms. Adventure's theory. If the gold ink would really react to the fragments, all we have to do is take our piece of the Lotus to his place, sneak inside while he's off getting his mind blown, and bing-bong-boom, we crack the case wide open!"

"You can't be serious." I snorted.

Selene stared at me, unblinking.

I threw my hands in the air and got off the couch. "Oh, sure. What's a little light breaking and entering on a Friday night?"

"You got any better ideas?"

I glanced at my watch. Only about thirty minutes had passed since we saw Mickey leave his apartment. There was no telling how long he would be … occupied. If we were going to do this, we needed to move fast.

Selene was smiling when I looked up from my wrist. "What?" I asked.

She hopped down from the couch, a victorious little bounce in her step. "I knew you couldn't resist. Now, come on, let's go!"

WE GOT to Mickey's apartment and Selene borrowed a drop of my magic to cast a hexing spell on the front door. The lock clicked open without any damage. We walked into the living room and carefully closed the door behind us.

I cast the cat a wary glance. "You sure did that awfully quickly."

"What?" Selene asked, all innocence and light. "I am good at hexes, what can I say?"

The apartment was quiet. All I could hear was the sound of my pulse pounding in my ears. I wiped my clammy hands on my jeans and then put on a pair of gloves. Selene would undoubtedly make fun of me, but I wasn't about to leave a bunch of fingerprints behind, on the off chance that Mickey was in fact tangled up in this bad business.

The place was clean. Maybe a little *too* clean. Like

serial killer clean. As if he was trying to hide something and always had to be at the top of his game.

"Where should we start?" Selene asked, her voice pitched with eagerness.

I shot her a quick scowl. "We should start by keeping our voices lower than that."

Selene held her tail high and strutted down the hallway.

It was dark outside, casting the apartment in shadows. I didn't want to risk turning on the overhead lights, so I tapped the flashlight feature on my phone and used it to get a lay of the land. The living room was separated from the kitchen and dining area by a structural wall. A well-worn brown couch lined one side of the living room, opposite a huge flat-screen TV, with a glass coffee table in the middle. There were no pictures hung on any of the walls, which were painted a bland eggshell white.

A pair of sneakers sat beside the front door, but other than that, there wasn't a trace of clutter anywhere. Even the kitchen was cleaned to within an inch of its life, without so much as a stray fork or plate in the dish rack. Apart from being freakishly clean, it looked like an average bachelor pad to me.

"There's a bookcase in here," Selene whispered from down the hall. "Let's get out the Lotus, see if it's doing anything."

I'd kept one hand protectively wrapped around the small bundle zipped in my front coat pocket since leaving Lavender's house. After we'd dug up the fragment of the Golden Lotus from Aunt Lavender's prepurchased cemetery plot, we'd kept it in a magically warded hideaway in her house. We didn't want to risk anyone noticing the freshly overturned dirt at the plot.

Exhaling a shaky breath, I unzipped my pocket and removed the top half of the Lotus before heading down the short hallway.

Selene gestured toward the bookcase with her tail. "Maybe he's got the pages hidden in one of these books. Is it doing anything? Getting warmer? Glowing?"

I shook my head and looked down at the golden petals. "Not yet, anyway."

"Maybe get closer," Selene hissed.

I shuffled forward. Still nothing.

Selene led me through the room, sweeping every nook and cranny as though we were on some kind of spy show looking for electronic bugs in a hotel room.

The Lotus remained unchanging.

"We don't even know what's supposed to happen," I hissed. "Or if this will even work. It was just a theory, remember?"

"Shh," Selene snapped. "Just give it another minute."

Panic started to rise in my chest, all the way until it hit the base of my throat.

"Maybe there's some kind of spell or something. Do you think—" My question was cut short by the sound of footsteps. Footsteps that sounded way too close.

The security light outside the front door flicked on, illuminating the silhouette of a man.

My heart froze in my chest and icy fear gripped my muscles, freezing them in place.

Selene's eyes went wide with horror as the dead bolt clicked.

Mickey was home!

16

"*B*athroom!" I hissed.

Selene bounded on silent feet, leaving me to scurry behind. I climbed into the bathtub-shower combo and yanked the curtain closed.

"Cora, the light!" Selene whispered.

A jolt of panic hit me in the chest with the impact of a fist. My fingers fumbled as I stuffed the Lotus fragment in my pocket and killed the flashlight on my phone.

Footsteps sounded in the living room. Then the door closed. I squeezed my eyes shut. I couldn't bear to look. We were going to get busted. It was only a matter of time.

We listened to Mickey moving around in the house. It sounded like he was alone. He wasn't talking to anyone, and I could only hear a single set of footsteps.

After a couple of agonizing moments, I glanced down at Selene. "We need to find a way to get out of here," I whispered. "He's going to come in here."

Selene poked her head around the edge of the curtain. "What about the window over the porcelain throne?"

I peeked around the other end of the curtain. "It's way too small," I replied, unsure whether I should be flattered she even thought I could fit. "Birthing hips, remember?" I muttered with a roll of my eyes.

"Now is not the time for a pity party, Cora." Selene hissed back. "Let me out the window. I'll go make a distraction outside so you can get away."

I considered the window. "I'm not sure that's the best idea."

"Okay then, what's your bright idea?" Selene's voice dripped with irritation.

I tried to think on my feet, but nothing sounded as good as Selene's suggestion. I gave her a stern look. "Okay, but *please* be careful, alright?"

Selene's whiskers twitched. "Oh *please*. I know what I'm doing."

Famous last words.

The sound of the TV blared to life, nearly giving me a heart attack. I sprang out of the tub, darted to the window, and threw it open. A screen blocked Selene's path, but with a soft blast of air magic it popped out of place and fell the three stories to the ground below.

I gulped and looked at Selene. Her eyes were large

as she followed the path of the fallen window screen. "Do you trust me?" I asked.

She glanced up at me. "I suppose I don't have a choice."

I nodded. "Jump. I'll break your fall. But you have to go now."

Our gaze locked for a long moment, then the cat exhaled and took a swan dive out the window. I shot a jet of air magic after her, providing an updraft strong enough to slow her down. Only once I was sure she'd landed safely on the ground did I retreat to the bathtub.

It didn't take long before I heard Selene. A loud caterwauling cry cut through the TV noise. I clapped a hand over my mouth to keep from laughing. Howls and yowls followed, then I heard something slam against the side of the apartment.

Furious footsteps thundered across the floor, and I crept out of my hiding place. It seemed Selene's plan was working.

The front door opened, and Mickey shouted, "Hey, get back here! That's mine!"

I made a break for it, fighting every instinct as I forced myself to leave the bathroom. I pressed my back against the wall and took tiny sideways steps as I moved down the hallway toward the front door.

Something else hit the wall and I winced. Mickey let out a string of colorful words. "You damn cat! Get out of here!"

Peeking around the corner, I saw the door was open.

Selene spotted me and took off down the stairs, dragging something in her mouth. Was that a welcome mat?

Mickey took the bait and began chasing Selene down the stairs. I waited just a few moments, then made my escape. I jogged down the first flight of steps, my heart in my throat, then down the second set. I pivoted to the right and ran—

Straight into Mickey's chest.

"Ahh!" I yelped, bouncing backward.

Confusion quickly bloomed into recognition and Mickey grabbed for my arms. "You! What are you doing here?"

"Dropped my keys earlier." Dodging left, I turned and ran. "Gotta go!"

My lungs burned in protest as I forced them to draw in as much oxygen as possible as I raced across the apartment's grounds.

Just make it to the car. Just make it to the car.

Selene was already there, sitting on the hood. "Let's go, let's go!"

"Thank goodness you made it," I said, panting as I fumbled to unlock the driver's side door. "How am I so out of shape? I go hiking all the time."

"Selene jumped in, bounced off my lap, and landed in the passenger seat. I jammed the key into the ignition and peeled out of the lot.

Only once I'd driven through three traffic stops did I finally loosen my grip on the steering wheel. I cut a glance over at Selene. "That's the last time I ever listen to any of your big ideas."

"Don't blame *me*," she replied with a scowl. "We really should be talking about the man's lack of control. By the goddess. You'd have thought being with an older woman would have taught him a thing or two!"

I stared at her, agog. "*That's* what you're worried about?"

Selene lifted her chin. "I'm merely making an observation."

I raked my fingers through my hair. It was a wonder that anything coming out of her mouth could shock me, and yet, she still pulled it off from time to time.

"We need to go back to Lavender's house and hide the Lotus," Selene said as I rolled to a stop at a four-way intersection.

"Right." I hit my blinker, indicating a right turn, then pulled forward.

When I turned onto Aunt Lavender's street, Selene shot upright like a jack in the box, her paws flattening against the passenger window. "Stop the car!"

"We're almost there," I replied, frowning as I maneuvered around a car parked on the side of the narrow road.

"There was something moving on the side of

Lavender's house," Selene said, her nose pressed to the glass.

"Are you sure it wasn't just a squirrel or something?" I narrowed my eyes and peered in that direction, slowing the car to a crawl as my aunt's dark bungalow came into view.

"Hardly a squirrel unless this one fell into a vat of nuclear waste and grew to about five times its original size."

"All right, just calm down," I sighed. "We'll investigate. Let me park the dang car first."

"Park on the street, not in the driveway," Selene instructed. "Or you may scare them off."

I still wasn't convinced that Selene had seen anything other than an animal darting around the side of the house, but to err on the side of caution—and avoid yet another argument—I appeased her and parked on the opposite side of the street.

The house appeared undisturbed, even better than before Aunt Lavender's disappearance, thanks to my brother taking over landscaping duties. If someone strolled through the neighborhood, they wouldn't even know that something truly terrible had happened here, or that the owner of the home was missing.

A *crack* of magic sounded, and the passenger door flew open. Selene darted out into the night, without hesitation.

"Selene!" I shouted. "What on *Earth* do you think you're doing?"

She ignored me as she bounded across the street, not giving me so much as a glance over her shoulder.

I groaned as I pushed the driver door open and climbed out of the car, scurrying to follow her.

"There they are again!" Selene exclaimed, picking up her pace as she rushed across the yard in pursuit of the unidentified culprit whom I could now see was a person and most definitely not a squirrel, or any other animal for that matter.

Selene disappeared around the corner of Aunt Lavender's house. I struggled to dig my phone out of my coat pocket and by the time I got the flashlight on, Selene had tackled the trespasser and had them pinned to their back in the middle of the yard, face down, with their arms and legs splayed out like a starfish.

"I hit them with a spell and knocked 'em right to the ground!" Selene crowed. "I've still got it!"

"All right, champ, now move so we can see who this is," I said, shooing the cat away.

Selene jumped off the person's back and they rolled over. A sheet of silvery-mauve hair fell aside, revealing Tabitha's face.

I gasped as I jumped back a step, nearly dropping my phone. "T—Tabitha? What the heck are you doing here?"

Selene growled, her fur standing on end.

Tabitha sat up and brushed a few leaves from her hair.

"What's going on?" I demanded. "Tabitha, tell us

what you're doing in my Aunt Lavender's backyard without permission."

"I can explain!" she said, holding up one hand. She reached around to her back with the other and rubbed at a spot in the middle. "That spell sure packed a wallop. It feels like the time I got shot in my Kevlar vest."

Selene flashed her fangs. "There's more where that came from if you don't start talking."

"Okay. Okay. I came over here to get something that belonged to Lavender to use for the tracking spell I have planned."

I crossed my arms. "And you didn't think to give us a heads-up? Or, better yet, ask for permission? Listen, Tabitha, I know you're here to help us, but this is still crossing a line. You can't just help yourself to my aunt's things. Her home."

Tabitha's face drained of color, her features etched with guilt. "You're right. I'm sorry." She exhaled as she pushed to her feet. Once upright, she rubbed at her back again. "I have a bad habit of getting tunnel vision when I'm working on a quest," she continued. "I get so caught up in what I'm doing that I bulldoze over boundaries and red tape."

I met her gaze. She seemed sincere, but there was a niggling of doubt in my stomach that wouldn't go away.

"It won't happen again," she promised. "I swear."

"Good."

Tabitha winced. "This really hurts. I'm going to head back to my hotel and take a soak in some Epsom salts."

For a moment I thought about stopping her, but we couldn't tell her about our escapades at Mickey's apartment. At least, not without confessing we had one half of the Golden Lotus, something that seemed even more unwise in the aftermath of her near break-in attempt.

So, I let her go. She offered a pained wave and a promise to check in the following day, then shuffled to her rented SUV, rubbing her back every few steps.

Selene marched back to stand beside me. "What do you think is going on with her?"

I shook my head, dumbfounded by the whole event. "I honestly have no idea."

"She was certainly acting peculiar."

"That's one way to put it."

Selene tilted her head and studied me. "Do you believe her story?"

I hesitated, watching Tabitha drive away. "I don't know. But I *want* to."

"I think we'd better keep the Lotus and the book at your place for now," Selene said. "I know a spell we can do to keep them both safe from prying eyes."

"Great minds think alike," I replied. "I'll go and get the book."

It took me a few minutes to retrieve Obin's Odyssey from its hiding place in my aunt's house. Then I rejoined Selene out front and led the way back to the car. "Come on, let's go home. I think we've earned some ice cream. I have a pint of cookies 'n' cream in the freezer."

"And this time, don't forget the whipped cream," Selene said, trailing closely on my heels. "I've had a very stressful evening."

17

"*H*ave you talked to Tabitha lately?" Selene asked.

I wiped my mouth with my napkin and shook my head, reaching for another slice of vegetarian-style pizza from the delivery box. "No, not since that encounter at Aunt Lavender's. For all I know, she's tucked her tail and gone home."

Selene briefly glanced up from the slab of seared tuna she'd been noshing on. "Well, if that's the case, then I say good riddance. What good did she do anyway? Sure, she found the so-called Golden Lotus expert, but you'll notice she didn't offer us his information so we could contact him directly."

"I suppose I could try texting her again. Or maybe stop by the hotel where she's been staying, see if she checked out." I crossed my legs and took a bite from the end of my pizza, my gaze wandering out the window into the night sky. The stars weren't very bright tonight, but the October moon hung low, a silvery crescent that pierced through the darkness.

"Forget about her, Cora." Selene shook her head, then tore off another piece of flaky fish. "We'll have Warden Quinton's ear soon enough."

I brightened ever so slightly. That bit of news was the highlight of the past week. We'd received word that Warden Quinton had agreed to meet with us on her trip to Winterspell. The warden's time was short, but we at least had our foot in the door.

"We should start working on our presentation," I said, lifting my slice. "And we need to be on the same page. We can't be talking over one another."

Selene puffed out her chest. "I tend to agree. I'm glad you think I should be our official spokesperson."

I frowned. That wasn't what I had in mind, but I wasn't going to argue with her. Things had more or less gone back to normal between Selene and me, but we weren't all that far removed from the ugly conversation we'd had after our fight in the storeroom.

Besides, Selene was just as invested in finding Aunt Lavender as I was. She knew the facts of the case inside and out. Plus, while she generally viewed everyone as a step or two beneath her, I had a feeling she would grant Warden Quinton the respect she deserved.

"That's fine with me," I said.

Selene blinked. She'd clearly been expecting pushback.

"What?" I asked before taking another bite.

Her eyes narrowed. "Don't tell me you've given up, Cora."

"Given up? What are you *talking* about?" I set my plate in my lap and wiped my fingers on a paper napkin. "Of course I haven't."

"I know things went sideways with Tabitha," Selene replied, "but this is different. Warden Quinton has real power."

I shook my head. "Why are you explaining this to me like I'm five years old? I know who Warden Quinton is and what she can do."

Selene canted her head. "Then why are you letting me do the presentation? You always fight me on things like that."

I sighed. "Because believe it or not, I think you'll do a good job. And I wanted to show you that I trust you."

The cat's suspicion only grew, her eyes turning to tiny blue slits. Her tail swished back and forth like a metronome.

"I'm serious!" I said, unable to hold back a laugh at the sheer absurdity of it all. "You can drop the fuzzy lie detector act, all right?"

"Hmm." Selene kept an eye on me as she went about taking another bite of her dinner. "You've been acting weird lately, you know."

"There's just been a lot going on. Things at the shop are getting better, but business is still a little slower than normal, and my lease rate is going up starting in

January. Aunt Lavender is still missing, despite our countless hours of work. I'm worried about her. I'm worried about my mom."

With a sigh, I set my plate on the table beside the couch. "Then there's been this mess with Tabitha. I honestly don't know what to think about that whole thing. The cynical part of me wonders if she was only coming to help so she could get into Aunt Lavender's house. You and I both know there's tons of treasure hunt trophies in there. Maybe there was something Tabitha had her heart set on and pretending to help us was her way of gaining access to the horde."

Selene dipped her chin, silently awarding me the point.

"And then … there's Clint." My heart clenched at the mere mention of his name. We hadn't spoken in days. Normally, he was the first one I called when anything happened with regard to the hunt for Aunt Lavender.

"You know, there's an old saying the witches in your family used to use," Selene told me.

I sat up a little straighter. Despite Selene's extensive history with the Hearth family witches, she never really talked much about her past guardians, the ones before Aunt Lavender.

"They'd say, either kill the frog or tip out the cauldron."

I frowned. "Kill the frog?"

Selene rolled one shoulder, her feline version of a shrug. "Modern magic has come a long ways. Back in the old days, some part of a frog went in tons of different potions, and the fresher the better, so … when a witch got squeamish, they'd say kill the frog or dump out the cauldron."

"Aha." I nodded, very grateful that even in my school biology classes we'd had a humane option for learning the various body systems without gutting a formaldehyde-marinated amphibian.

I tipped my head to one side, considering the cat's words of wisdom. "And this pertains to me and Clint how, exactly? Is he the frog … or the cauldron?"

Selene gave a long-suffering sigh. "He's not a frog or a cauldron! The point is, get on with it. Make a decision and live with it, one way or the other. All this hemming and hawing isn't getting you anywhere."

"I see. So, your advice is to rip off the Band-Aid. To use a more modernized version of the expression."

"That implies pain," Selene countered. "You have two choices. One is to cut the man loose. That would be the so-called Band-Aid ripping, I suppose. The other is to give up your need to control everything and let the road lead where it leads."

"You think this is about me wanting to control the situation?" I asked, my brows furrowed.

"You don't?" The cat sounded honestly flabbergasted. "Oh, Cora. We have so much work to do. What's your health insurance like? Any chance you can go get your head shrunk from time to time? It might do you some good."

"Knock it off." I scowled. "Let's play pretend here. Say I continue things with Clint. Say things go really well and six months from tonight, he sweeps me away on some romantic beach weekend, or something like that, and one night at dinner, he gets down on one knee and pops the question. How am I supposed to know whether it's because he truly wants to marry me, and not that he's run out of money and needs his trust fund?"

"There wouldn't be a way to know beyond a shadow of a doubt," Selene said, her tone blunt. "It comes down to trust. Do you trust that Clint is an honest man, with honest intentions?"

My lips sealed closed. I wanted to say yes, but there was something holding me back.

"Well, then there you go," Selene said after a moment. "If you don't trust him, you have no business getting in deeper. So, then, yes. Grab that Band-Aid and pull, cupcake."

I shot the cat a sidelong glare. "What have I said about the whole *cupcake* thing?"

Selene took a bite of tuna.

"I suppose you're right. I just wish it didn't have to be this way. But I think, especially after everything that happened in my first marriage, I can't risk things going sideways again. Maybe I have trust issues. Maybe even some control issues."

Selene nearly choked on her tuna. "Some?"

"You know what, I have a saying for you," I said, my

tone heated. "It goes like this: those who live in glass houses shouldn't throw stones. Or, here's another one: pot meet kettle! You've got control issues yourself, missy. Everything has to be just so. The thermostat setting, the temperature and plating of your food, the brand of litter in your overpriced robot box. You have to read the newspaper before me, even though half the time you end up smudging the ink with your wet paws from going out in the rain to fetch it, making it unreadable by the time you *allow* me to take a page. On and on and on it goes!"

Selene's ears went flat against her head. "All right, first off, I do not *fetch* anything. I am a cat. Not a dog."

I threw my hands into the air. "This is ridiculous. Let's change the subject. I don't want to argue with you."

"Fine by me."

A loud *buzz* sounded from the kitchen, and I jumped off the couch to grab my phone. "Saved by the bell," I muttered to myself as I rounded the corner. The number on the screen was local, but there was no name attached to the caller ID.

"Uh, hello?" I answered.

"Hello," a male voice replied. "Is this Cora Hearth?"

"It is. Can I help you?"

"Oh, good. This is James Midnight. Do you have a moment?"

"Of course. What's up?"

I knew Selene would be dying of curiosity—being a

cat and all—but I didn't bother peeking around the corner to tell her who was on the other end of the line.

"It's probably nothing, but I was looking through my appointment book earlier today, and it jogged a memory. About six weeks ago I met with another young woman, probably around your age, and she was asking about secured vaults. Like I told you, they've intensive, high-labor jobs, so I don't get too many requests for them. But anyway, this woman asked a lot of the questions you did, about how the mechanics worked, whether or not items could be secured, how the binding spells worked."

"Did she end up booking a job with you?" I asked, already assuming the answer was *no*.

"She thanked me for my time and said she would think about it, but she never came back again. I didn't think much of it at the time, but in light of what you told me, I thought maybe it might be connected somehow."

"Well, thank you. I appreciate the information. Could I ask what her name was?"

"I've only got her first name written here in my appointment book. It's Mona. You might ask my daughter, Jasmine, if she remembers her last name."

"They knew each other?" I asked.

"Seemed to. Jasmine came in when I was meeting with Mona. She manages the bakery now that I've started my own business, and she needed me to sign off on the payroll. Anyway, she and Mona acted like they were old classmates or something."

"Right." I bobbed my head. "Okay. Thanks. I might do that. Thanks again for calling, Mr. Midnight."

"Of course. Good night, Cora."

"Night."

I hung up the call and stared at the phone screen, leaving Selene to stew in suspense.

"You're being petty," the cat called after a long moment. "Just tell me what that was all about."

With a flick of my eyes up toward the ceiling, I pushed away from the counter and joined Selene in the living room. Plopping on the couch, I held up the phone. "That was James Midnight. He said about six weeks ago he had a consultation with a woman named Mona. She was asking about secured vaults and binding spells, sort of like we did."

Selene frowned. "That's it?"

I shrugged. "I guess he thought it strange to have two people asking about them within a short span of time. Secured rooms and vaults aren't his specialty, so he doesn't do many of them, or advertise those services."

"I see. And does this Mona have a last name?"

"He didn't know it, but said his middle daughter, Jasmine, might have gone to school with her. I'm not sure how old Jasmine is, but she's a few years younger than Rosella, his oldest daughter, and she was four years behind me in academy." I straightened, my palms slapping my thighs as I sprang off the couch. "I have an idea!"

I raced down the hall, to my spare room-slash-guest room-slash-Selene's private bathroom-slash-storage space. I had a tall bookcase wedged in one corner. Most of the shelves were covered in random candle-making supplies, overflow from what I could fit in Wicked Wicks' storeroom. But the bottom three shelves had paperbacks, family photo albums, scrapbooks I'd made as a teen, and a set of yearbooks from the Winterspell Academy.

Selene followed me into the room and leaped onto the desk that was also covered in supplies and notebooks. She scowled as she made a show of carefully stepping over the obstacles to find a level place to plant her fuzzy rear. "You're starting to turn into your aunt. I hope you know."

"Am not," I replied, already flipping through the yearbook from my final year of high school. The academy was large enough that everyone attended the same school, rather than having separate schools for different grade levels. Something of a magical K–12.

"Mona. Mona. Mona," I muttered, flipping through the younger grades. "Aha!" I pressed a finger to the photo of a smiling brunette with braces and glasses. "There's Jasmine Midnight. So, if they were in the same grade, Mona must be here somewhere…"

I moved my finger down the rows of smiling faces, until I saw it.

Mona Peters.

"Here she is," I said, flashing a triumphant smile. Then recognition hit and I gasped.

"What?!" Selene pounced from her perch, landing with a soft *thump* on the carpeted floor beside me. "What is it, Cora?"

I jabbed my finger at the photo. "It's her! The blonde!"

Selene leaned in for a closer look, then let out a low whistle—something I didn't know she could anatomically manage.

The smiling girl in the photo was a younger, slightly awkward version of the curvy blonde we'd caught Mickey with a few nights ago.

Selene flashed her dainty canines. "Well, well, well, looks like good ole Mickey just might have something to do with this after all."

18

"*Y*up. It's official. We're going to jail tonight."

Selene shot me a scowl from her place in the passenger seat. "Oh, hush up. You can't go getting cold feet now."

I glanced down at my all-black attire. "I feel like a cat burglar."

Selene scrunched her nose. "Why would anyone want to burgle a cat?"

"Beats me," I quipped, then sighed as the moment of amusement faded. "You're sure this is the right move?"

Selene placed her paws on the window. Across the street was the blue-and-white house where Mona, presumably, lived. "It's the best lead we've found so far."

I frowned as I peered over at the house. The exterior lights were on, but the windows were dark. The house had a one-car garage attached to it, but the door was closed and there weren't any cars in the driveway. "I just don't get what Mona's possible connection is to this."

Granted, with our limited resources we hadn't been able to find much on the woman in general. If we had Tabitha on our side, maybe she could have found something, the way she had with Mickey. But she hadn't answered my phone call, and I wasn't in the mood to beg for any more of her attention.

All we knew was Mona and Mickey had a thing going. If she was the woman Bernadette told us about, then she'd met Mickey at his brother's bachelor party. Although, that could have just been a story Mickey fed Bernadette in an attempt to gain her forgiveness for cheating. Or, Mona could be another woman entirely. I'd personally never dealt with a cheating boyfriend, but I had plenty of friends who had, and it didn't seem there was really a *type* for it. For all we knew, Mickey had a rotation of women on his speed dial.

"Look, let's just slip into the backyard and check to see if the Lotus does anything," Selene said, breaking into my thoughts before I could fully talk myself out of the whole plan. "If nothing happens, we'll go home and do some more digging. Maybe we can go talk to the Midnight girl over at Sugar Shack. She might know something."

I nodded, though my pulse ticked up another few beats per minute as I reached for the key and turned off the car's engine.

Selene led the way, streaking across the street so fast I doubted anyone would even notice her. I didn't have the advantage of a dark fur coat and four legs, so I took a different approach. I pulled my phone out of my pocket and walked down the sidewalk a ways before crossing over to Mona's side of the street. If any of her neighbors happened to look out their front windows, they'd likely assume I was out for an evening stroll—granted, a risky one, considering my all-black getup.

When I dared to cross the street and approach Mona's yard, I glanced up. No one was outside and most of the homes that were lit up had TV screens on. I drew in a breath and told myself no one would even notice me. Then I turned and scurried to the chain-link gate, leading to the fenced portion of the home's small yard.

"What's taking so long?" Selene hissed.

"Just let me do this my way, all right?"

She scoffed but didn't admonish me further. I chalked it up as a slight win.

"I'll get the Lotus," I said, digging into the front pocket of my hoodie sweatshirt. My usual coat was a powder blue, not at all suitable for stealth, and after our close encounter at Mickey's apartment, I wouldn't be wearing it for snooping anytime soon.

"Ouch!" I yelped as my fingers brushed the hard lump of metal. "This thing feels like it's on fire!"

Selene's eyes glowed. "It's working?"

I paused to put on a glove before removing the fragment of the Lotus from my pocket. It glowed as bright as a torch, the light seeming to heat the golden exterior.

I dragged my eyes away from it and looked to Selene. The cat's jaw hung open. "Selene?" I said, my voice quivering. "What—what do we do now?"

Selene raced to the back door. "We go inside and find those pages! They must be here somewhere!"

Adrenaline surged through my veins, and somewhere deep down, the last spark of hope I'd extinguished came bursting to life again. We were in the right place. I felt it with every fiber of my existence.

Crack.

A flurry of pink sparks snapped my attention away from the glowing shard of the Lotus, and I looked up just in time to see Selene blast her way through Mona's back door—using my magic.

"Selene!" I barked. "What have I said about—"

From somewhere inside the house, a scream pierced the air.

Selene reared back from the open doorway, her eyes flashing. "Oopsies! Guess maybe someone is home after all."

With a growl, I shoved the Lotus back into my hoodie pocket. "Gee, ya think?"

A figure appeared, but it wasn't Mona. It was Mickey.

His eyes were huge as the recognition clicked into place, his gaze panning between me and Selene. "Hey!

You're the witch who broke into my apartment!" He leered at us, marching forward with his fists balled in anger. "What are you doing here?"

As he lumbered out onto the small back porch, Mona stepped into the doorway, her arms crossed over her busty chest. She wore a silky robe, and judging by Mickey's bare torso and the low-riding pair of sweatpants clinging to his hips, we'd interrupted a romantic evening in.

I cringed. We should have peeked through the garage window. Though, how I could have done so and maintained a low profile was beyond me.

"Oh, good, you're both here," Selene said, not a hint of a quiver in her voice. But then, that was her superpower. Where most beings had a healthy dose of fear and common sense, the pint-sized cat had bravado and recklessness.

Maybe she wasn't pulling my leg with this whole ninth-life business after all.

"We know you stole the pages about the Golden Lotus," Selene continued, her glower intensifying as she stared at the pair of them.

"*That's* what this is about?" Mickey tossed his head. "I told you, I don't know anything about it. Sal told me he had the book, but that was it. I never saw it, touched it, nothing."

Selene's icy stare shifted to Mona.

The color drained from her pretty face. Her blonde hair was pulled up in a messy bun, exposing her slender neck and part of her chest—which was now blotched with red. "I don't know what you're talking about. I don't even know who you are."

"One of you is lying," I said, my hand slipping back into my pocket to grip the Lotus. We couldn't tell them we had it. That would be too dangerous. But maybe there was another way to flush out the truth. "We have the rest of the book."

Selene snapped around to stare at me, her tail ramrod straight.

My throat constricted. I swallowed hard and continued. There was no turning back now. "My Aunt Lavender got it from Salvatore before he died. Perhaps you met her," I said, fixating on Mickey. "Lavender Hearth. She was an old friend and client of Sal's."

Mickey frowned. "He sometimes hung out with an old lady. Wild hair, Coke-bottle glasses, wore a lot of muumuus?"

"Witches robes!" Selene hissed.

"Obin put a spell in his book," I lied. "One that could be used if any pages ever went missing. We cast that spell tonight, and it led us here."

I sucked in a breath, holding it until Mickey's expression shifted from anger to confusion. "That— that doesn't make any sense. This is my girlfriend's house, and she—" He stopped, a muddle of doubt creeping over his face. He adjusted his glasses and cast a sidelong glance at Mona.

She shrank back half a step, into the dark interior of the house.

My eyes widened as I followed his gaze. "We know you spoke to James Midnight," I said, loud enough that she could hear. "You were asking questions about Sal's vault."

"What?" Mickey's brow furrowed. He reached into the house and tugged Mona out by the arm. It wasn't violent, but firm enough that Mona didn't try to wrench herself away. "Mona, what is she talking about? Is this true?"

"I—can explain. It's just..." Mona trailed off, wringing her fingers together. She gave Mickey a tortured look. She might not care about what *we* thought, but it was clear she was desperately seeking his approval.

Mickey's eyes remained hard. "What did you do, Mona?"

"I did it for you!" Mona cried, her voice wobbling with panic. "I did it for us!"

Selene bolted past the woman's legs, not bothering to wait around for the full explanation. "Come on, Cora! They're here somewhere!"

Mona yelped and hurried after the cat. Mickey ran after Mona.

"Selene!" I exclaimed, rushing after all three of them.

Mickey threw on an overhead light, and I spotted Selene rooting around the oak entertainment center. A flat-screen TV sat flanked by two bookshelves that held a handful of knickknacks.

"Get away from there!" Mona shouted, her eyes wide, like a scared animal.

The Lotus grew warmer in my concealed clutch. "It's around here somewhere, Selene."

"Just leave! This is none of your business!" Mona said, her voice cracking on the last word.

"What is going *on?*" Mickey demanded.

Selene swiped her paw at a small, brown, wooden box and sent it flying to the ground.

Mona gasped as the force of the impact knocked the lid off, and a folded wad of old papers fell across the area rug. A half howl, half growl escaped from her throat, and she fell to her knees, her arms outstretched, hands grabbing to snatch up the pages.

"Mona, what have you done?" Mickey's voice was horror-struck as he watched her.

She had this ominous, possessive glaze in her eyes that sent a shiver down my spine.

Mickey pulled her away from the pages, then glanced at me and gave a small, begrudging nod, allowing me to collect them. I handled them carefully. Having never seen the missing content, I couldn't one hundred percent guarantee the writing and small illustrations matched the rest of Obin's tome.

Mona turned into Mickey's chest and began to sob, her thin body shaking with the sheer force of her emotions.

Mickey's jaw flexed as his arms hung at his side. He didn't step away from her, but all affection of a romantic partner had vanished from his face. "Why did you do this?"

"I wanted to make you happy," Mona squeaked, her eyes pleading with him.

"Happy?" Mickey's features warped with disgust. He bared his teeth, his eyes flashing with fury as he backed away from her. "You desecrated a major historical work, Mona! This goes against everything I stand for."

"Mickey—" Mona reached for him. "You were the one who told me how much money these pages were worth!"

Mickey's eyes blazed hot and wild. "Don't you dare try and pin this on me. I had *nothing* to do with this."

Mona's bottom lip stuck out as fresh tears filled her eyes. "I was going to tell you about it when the time was right. I thought we could sell them and finally buy a house, like we always talk about. Go on a nice trip, or something."

"A—a *trip*?" Mickey's mouth dropped open.

Mona blinked away her tears. "It's just a stupid old book. What difference does it make?" she asked, a defiant edge to her tone.

Mickey held up his hands and turned to walk away. "I can't deal with you right now."

He stepped outside through the back door, leaving us to deal with Mona.

"Men!" she scoffed.

I held up the pages. "Mona, tell us what happened."

She crossed her arms as she spun back around to face me. Her tears had magically dried up. "Sometimes I'd go and visit Mickey at that old man's house—or, his castle, is more like it." She scoffed. "That's the thing. He's acting all broken up about this, but that old guy has a billion books. He's never going to notice a few pages have gone missing!"

Selene looked up at me, stunned. "She can't be this dense, can she?"

"Hey!" Mona squealed.

"Mona, we're here because of those missing pages," I explained. "So, clearly someone noticed."

The blonde flapped a hand. "Whatever."

"And Salvatore Greco is deceased now," I added, barely constraining my growing frustration.

She shrugged. "He was *really* old."

Selene growled.

"Why did you take the pages?" I asked, hurrying to continue the conversation before Selene sank her claws into the woman's ankles. "You said you did it for you and Mickey. You were planning to sell them. But why that particular book? And why these particular pages?"

"Mickey was always talking about it. He said it would help in his research for the book he's writing, but he could never afford the asking price, and the old man was being stingy. He wouldn't even let him borrow it." Mona shifted her weight and adjusted the sash on her robe. "I finally got tired of listening to him talk about it, so I went to the house one day when Mickey was at work. I thought maybe I could … work my charms, so to speak."

"Oh, boy. This oughta be good," Selene muttered.

Mona ignored the cat's snarky commentary. Unbothered, she continued. "I pretended I was interested in seeing his collection. He brought out a bunch of books for me to look at, but I didn't see the one Mickey wanted. I finally got tired of hinting and asked him outright for Oden's book."

"*Obin*," I corrected.

Mona rolled her eyes. "Whatever. The old man said he didn't know what I was talking about, and he thought I should leave. I asked to use the powder room before I left." A smile plucked at the corners of her lips. "He left me to it, and I followed him back to the library and watched him open that secret passageway."

"What happened next?"

"He came out and I asked him a bunch of questions about it. He didn't want to tell me anything at first, but then I asked him who designed it, because I was looking to add a shoe closet but didn't have the square footage in my house. He told me to talk to James Midnight. Then I let him walk me to the door."

"So, you went to see James and asked how the vault worked," I said. It was a statement more than a question, but Mona nodded along. "But that doesn't explain how you got those pages."

"I'm getting to that part," Mona said impatiently. "I

knew I couldn't get the whole book out of the vault, not with the magic spell on it, but I thought I could probably get *some* of it. And from what Mickey told me in one of his rambling lectures, there was only one part that people would pay for—the part about this golden lily or something."

I sighed. For a woman who had gone to such lengths to get the pages, she sure didn't have her facts straight.

"Anyway, I went to the library a few days later. There were always too many people about during the day, so when it got close to the time people usually left, I slipped into one of the guest rooms down the hall and hid, waiting for everyone else to leave. After that, all I had to worry about was that nosy little maid that followed Mickey around like a lost puppy dog."

"You mean his *other* girlfriend?" Selene interjected.

Mona barked a laugh. "You can't be serious!"

I leveled the woman with a harsh stare. "Bernadette and Mickey were together, romantically. She told us so herself."

Mona waved a hand. "In her dreams, maybe."

Mickey reappeared in the doorway, his face expressionless. "It's true, Mona."

The smile slid off Mona's face. "W—what? Mickey, you can't be—she isn't—"

"I was seeing her long before I met you," he interjected. "She ended things a few days ago, after you got drunk and tagged me in one of your Instagram stories, showing me asleep in your bed the morning after Ben's bachelor party."

Selene laughed. "This is like a real-life episode of *Love Island*, huh, Cora?"

Mona's eyes went glacial. "You were *cheating* on me, this whole time?"

"Technically, I'd say I was cheating on Bernadette with you." There wasn't an ounce of remorse in Mickey's dead tone. "But that hardly matters. I may have lied about who I am, but you did, too. I never pegged you for a thief."

With her eyes locked on Mickey, Mona snapped her fingers and a burst of flames appeared, dancing on the palm of her hand. Without warning, she flicked her hand in my direction and the pages from Obin's tome caught fire.

"No!" I screamed, frantically trying to put out the flames before they could swallow the pages whole.

Mickey swore and ran at Mona. "Get out!" he shouted over his shoulder. "Get the pages away from here! Now!"

I smothered the last flame—thankful for my gloves—and bolted out the back door.

WE NEVER GOT the full story from Mona, but it wasn't too hard to put the remaining pieces together. She must have stayed hidden in the house, only sneaking back into the library after Bernadette went home. From there, all she had to do was open the vault— which she had seen Salvatore do on her previous scouting trip—and cut out the pages pertaining to the Golden Lotus. It seemed the only snag in her plan was that beyond Mickey, she didn't have any connection to the rare book world and had no idea how to go about finding a buyer for the pages. So, she'd stashed them in her house, biding her time while she worked out her next steps.

The specifics didn't matter much in the grand scheme of things. We now had one half of the Lotus and the missing pages to complete Obin's tome. We knew everything except the thing we wanted to know the most: Who took Aunt Lavender?

Mona was misguided and selfish, but it was clear she wasn't some kind of criminal mastermind. She wasn't capable of something as elaborate as kidnapping my aunt, nor did she have a motive to do so.

Which meant, yet again, Selene and I were back at the drawing board.

So, when Tabitha breezed into my candle shop the following morning, neither one of us was all that thrilled to see her. Her appearance was something like salt in our freshly opened wounds.

I got Lily's attention from across the store and

gestured for her to step in and finish with the customer I'd been helping. We traded places and I approached the counter where Tabitha stood waiting. "Morning," she said, offering a soft smile. Her face was dolled up in her usual makeup. "Do you have a minute to talk?"

Selene came wandering in from the back room. Judging by the bleary look in her eyes, she'd only just woken up from a cat nap. She did a quick double take and her fur stood up on end. "What are *you* doing here?" she asked, jumping up onto the front counter.

"Let's hear her out," I said to the cat, running a hand down her back to smooth the ruffled fur back into place.

Selene cut me a sharp glare but didn't protest.

"I'm sorry I went radio silent on you," Tabitha began. "I was embarrassed, after what happened at Lavender's house the other night. To tell you the truth, I thought about leaving town. But I didn't feel good about that decision. I never give up on a quest. And this one is too important."

I inclined my head. "We appreciate that."

She placed her palm to her heart and gave me an endearing smile. "To make it up to you, I made some calls, and I have some good news."

"What is it?" Selene asked, still glowering at Tabitha.

"I've contacted a treasure hunter friend of mine. He used to work as a bounty hunter, before he decided that chasing *things* was safer than chasing people."

"Okay..."

"Anyway," Tabitha continued, her smile widening, "he's agreed to lend me a tracking pixie."

I gawked at her. "Wow, are you serious?"

Tracking pixies were extremely rare, but they worked much like a bloodhound or a German shepherd, used to search for missing people or clues in an investigation. On top of that, they could fly, giving them almost limitless access to pursue their targets.

Tabitha held up a hand. "It's still a bit of a long shot, considering how much time has passed since Lavender was taken. But these pixies are quite skilled. I think it's worth a shot if you're willing to try."

Selene and I exchanged a look. "We'll do anything if it could lead us to Lavender," Selene told Tabitha.

I nodded in agreement. "When will you get the pixie?"

Tabitha smiled. "In two days."

19

*B*efore our date with Tabitha and the tracking pixie, I had one with Clint. I'd put him on the back burner for long enough, and try as I might, I couldn't shake Selene's ridiculous colloquialism about frogs and cauldrons.

Unfortunately, I'd decided the pending conversation was better suited for a private venue, which meant Selene had front-row seats. She glanced at the clock on the wall. "What time is 'Mama's Boy' coming over, anyway?"

Frowning, I picked at the pilling on the sleeve of my sweater. "Don't call him that."

Selene flashed her teeth. "My other choice was Monopoly Man. Is that better?"

"Not even a little bit." I ran my fingers through my hair and peeked out the front window. "He should be here soon. So, what's it going to take to get you to scram?"

"Hmm. Let me think." She swished her tail as she mulled it over, her eyes glowing with the possibilities.

I braced myself.

"How about I get control of the remote for the rest of the month, you locate a pet massage therapist and book me their next appointment, and you spring for the premium version of that fishing game I like to play on your iPad. The ads are annoying."

I blinked. The first two requests didn't shock me. The third one caught me off guard. "You actually play that? I downloaded it as a joke."

Selene licked one paw and rubbed it over her whiskers. "I get bored sometimes. So sue me."

"But with your mind and intelligence, you really like slapping digital fish on a screen?"

Selene narrowed her eyes. "We got a deal or not, cupcake? Cause I'm pretty sure I just heard Clint's car pull up."

My eyes flew to the window and, sure enough, a black BMW was idling in the street, waiting for a car to pass before the path into my driveway was cleared.

"Okay! Okay, deal," I squeaked. "Now shoo!"

"All right." Selene stretched, then hopped down from the arm of the couch and sashayed out of the room. Moments later, I heard her cat flap slap shut.

I exhaled and went to the front door. "Frogs and cauldrons," I whispered. "Frogs and cauldrons."

Clint had just raised his hand to knock when I

swung the door open and greeted him. "Oh!" He smiled and held up a paper bag. "I come bearing gifts. I hope Italian is okay."

"Of course!" I took a step back and gestured for him to come inside. "Italian always sounds good."

Clint's eyes met mine as he hesitated in the entry-way. He started to reach for me with his free arm, then pulled back as I stepped forward. We both smiled, trying to break the tension.

"It's good to see you," I said, giving him a quick side hug.

He wore a white-and-blue plaid button-down shirt with the sleeves rolled up to the elbows. It was as casual as he ever got, save for his pajamas. He'd paired the button-up with dark-wash jeans and a pair of expensive-looking boots. His dark hair was slicked back with product. A whiff of cologne trailed after him as he made his way into the kitchen. The familiar scent made my heart ache. I was still hopelessly attracted to Clint. I wanted nothing more than to wrap my arms around him and get lost in a passionate kiss.

Clint placed the bag of takeout on my dining table and began unpacking the contents. "I got you eggplant parmesan. I know it's your favorite. And extra garlic bread. Obviously." He flashed me a smile and my stomach flip-flopped.

"Thanks. It smells delicious." I tucked a short tendril behind my ear and took my seat at the table.

Clint laid out the spread, ensuring we had the proper utensils and adequate napkins before he sat down in the chair opposite me. We smiled at each other, the silence heartbreaking. We used to be one of those couples that was always bursting to talk to each other at the end of the day. We'd find things to talk about even if we'd only been apart a few hours. Now, here we were, not having seen each other in days, and we had nothing to say.

Clint dug into his box of spaghetti carbonara. "Bon appétit," he said.

I cut into the piece of eggplant. It was expertly fried; the breaded exterior a pleasing golden-brown underneath a hearty helping of the vibrant marinara sauce.

"How is it?" Clint asked as I chewed.

I bobbed my head. "Really good. Thank you."

"Oh! I forgot the wine in the car." Clint dabbed his mouth with a napkin, then held up a finger to excuse himself. He dashed outside, returning a moment later with a bottle of cabernet. He didn't need to ask where I kept the corkscrew or the wineglasses. We'd had plenty of nights here, cuddled up on the couch with a movie, splitting a bottle of something while we munched through a bowl of popcorn.

The subtle reminder only deepened the knife tip poised against my heart.

Clint did his best to keep his placid smile in place as he set a glass before me. "There you go. I hope it's okay.

It was the best one I could find at the market. The selection there is surprisingly terrible."

I smiled and reached for the stem of the glass. "I'm sure it's fine. You know I'm not much of a sommelier."

Clint smiled as he retook his seat. "Right."

We ate a few more bites in strained silence, peeking at each other as we chewed or sipped our wine. The longer it went on, the more unbearable it became.

Finally, I couldn't take it anymore. I set my fork down and folded my hands in my lap. "Clint, can we please stop trying so hard?"

Clint set his glass down and wiped his mouth again. "I'm sorry, Cora. I guess I just don't know where you're at right now. I know we left things in a bit of an awkward spot the other night, after dinner."

I exhaled slowly through my nose, taking an extra beat to gather my thoughts. "All right, since I'm the one who suggested this dinner, I'll go first."

Clint sat at attention, his eyes sad, like he already knew what was coming next.

"In some ways, I feel like I've spent the past week on a merry-go-round," I told him. "The same thoughts keep spinning through my mind. The ride always stops at the same place—but it's not where I want to be. So, I spin through it all again and again, hoping for a different answer."

Clint looked down at his plate. His Adam's apple bobbed.

My cheeks warmed and a stinging sensation

prickled at my nose. "Clint, I really care about you. And if things were different, I wouldn't be saying any of this, but I think—" A tear slipped down my cheek, and I paused just long enough to swipe it away. "I think maybe we should end things here. The longer we drag it out, the harder it's going to be, and this is already really, *really* hard."

Clint looked up and met my gaze, his dark eyes glossy. "Cora, please, don't do this." He exhaled sharply, glancing past my shoulder for a long moment. "I wish you had never heard any of that stuff my mother said. That's what started all of this."

I stayed quiet, silently wishing the same thing. Sure, maybe that would have only prolonged the inevitable, but for tonight, I'd be blissfully unaware. We could be in each other's arms. Happy. If only for a little while longer.

"I'm going to talk to her," Clint said, meeting my gaze once more. "There is still time for her to change her mind."

"About the inheritance?" I asked.

Clint nodded.

Under the table I twisted my fingers together. "But Clint, even if you could change her mind about the inheritance, it doesn't change the fact that you don't feel like you belong here in Winterspell. It's too different from your life in Chicago."

Clint frowned. "I never said that. The only reason I'm considering going back is because of my job, Cora."

I canted my head. "So, you don't miss it? Tell the truth."

"At first I thought I could have the best of both worlds," Clint explained, his eyes reverting to his massive container of spaghetti. "I *welcomed* a slower-paced work experience, as opposed to the rat race I'd been weaving in and out of for so long."

"Right." I nodded. "But…?"

"It's a big change," Clint said. "Sure, I can text and call my old colleagues and friends, but it would be nice to spend time with them. I miss the variety. The restaurants, entertainment—" He gestured toward the bottle of wine. "I miss having a decent wine shop to go to."

"Well, then it sounds like your mind is made up." I didn't mean to sound bitter, but my lips twisted around the words, like they left a bad taste in my mouth.

"Cora, please, don't be like that," Clint said, his eyes pleading with me. "There are things I like about this place that I'd never find in Chicago. Like, seeing the stars at night. The walking trails and all of the greenery and beautiful sunrises over the lake."

He reached across the table, his palm spread wide.

My stomach swooped, and I reached for him, placing my hand in his.

"Things with my mother have gone so far off course," he continued, clutching my hand. "I didn't think it was possible, but somehow she's only grown more caustic since Seth died. I thought his death might soften her heart, and spur her to try and repair our relationship, but it seems to have had the opposite effect. Half the time when I go to visit her, she doesn't even say anything. Just sits in silence until I get tired of trying to kindle a conversation and leave. The days she speaks, it's mostly barbed insults or complaints about her household staff."

My heart clenched. "I'm sorry, Clint. That must be incredibly hard to deal with."

He nodded. "I've come to peace with it. At least, as much as I can." He squeezed my hand. "You've been the bright spot in my life in this whole mess. I've never fallen so hard, so fast, Cora. I love you."

Fresh tears welled up in my eyes. I blinked a few times, trying to clear them before they could slide down my cheeks. "I know," I said, the words clogged with emotion. "It's been fast for me, too. But that's part of what scares me, Clint. I'm afraid my heart is getting ahead of my brain."

"In what way?"

"Well, not to open the ex-files, but with Rodger, we started out with all of this stuff in common. It was so easy. Then, as the years went on, we just sort of lost touch. Grew apart. He wanted to leave Winterspell. He felt constrained by the small-town life. So, when he got a job opportunity outside of the magical world, he jumped at it. And when I didn't want to go with him … we decided it was best to separate. Permanently."

I swallowed the lump in my throat. "It happened slowly, over time. But somehow it still surprised me, you know? It was like we went from being inseparable, to virtual strangers, or at the very least, roommates, in a handful of years. And I can't—I can't go through that again. So, when you talk about how great Chicago is, and how much you miss it sometimes, I can't help but get flashbacks."

I sniffled. "That's why I said what I said. If you want to go back, I'd rather you go now. It will still hurt, of course, but it will be a lot less painful in the long run if we stop here. Cut our losses and move on as best we can."

"There's a difference though, Cora. I'm not Rodger." Clint's grip tightened on my hand. "I can be happy here in Winterspell. I'll find a new job. A new passion. Hey, maybe you'll convert me to an outdoorsman."

I snorted a laugh.

"I'm serious!" He smiled. "You know me. I'm not the type of guy who just sits around waiting for life to happen while it passes by me at warp speed."

"I know that. But what about the money?"

He paused and frowned. "I don't know. But for *you*, I'm willing to do what it takes. If that means quitting my consulting job and getting a job as a dishwasher at Whimzee's Deli, well, then so be it, I guess."

I shook my head as hot tears pricked behind my eyes. "No. I won't let you do that."

Clint's eyes searched mine. "Why not? I look good in an apron. You've told me that before, remember?" He smiled, but it faded all too quickly.

"I am not willing to be the reason you abandon your career and your goals. I'm not your prison warden, Clint. You are allowed to live your own life and make your own decisions. I won't allow that guilt to fall on my shoulders."

Clint blinked as he stared at me. "What guilt?"

"The guilt I'll feel when you eventually start to resent me because you feel anchored to Winterspell."

Clint's eyes glistened. "I won't feel resentment or anchored."

I closed my eyes and sighed before looking at him again. "Yes, you will."

Clint's eyes widened. "Cora—"

"No." I cut him off. He needed to hear this. "I'd always be the girl you gave up everything for, and that wouldn't be fair to either of us. You'd try to make it work, to justify your choices. And I'd try to make it work out of guilt for holding you back. It's too much pressure."

He opened his mouth to protest but I pulled my hand back from his before I changed my mind. "No, Clint. Don't."

"I don't want this to end," he said, his voice a hoarse whisper.

I could barely see him through the pool of tears blurring my vision. "I don't either, but I don't see this ending any other way."

Clint's features crumbled. "I can't change your mind?"

Slowly, I shook my head. "I'm so sorry, Clint."

He held my gaze for another heart-wrenching moment, then slowly stood up from the table. He leaned over and kissed me gently, an overwhelming swell of emotions poured into the way our lips met. And then he straightened, gave me a sad, pained smile, and left.

e met Tabitha in Aunt Lavender's front yard exactly two hours later. Tabitha smiled at our approach. She wore her usual black boots with a pair of dark skinny jeans and the bomber jacket she'd had on the day we first met. Her hair was tied up in a long ponytail, and while she had on her signature smoky eye and red lipstick, there was something different about her, almost a little less polished than usual.

I parked beside her rental in Aunt Lavender's driveway and exhaled. "Here goes … everything," I said quietly to Selene.

Selene gave an almost imperceptible nod, then jumped out of the car.

I cut the engine and joined her and Tabitha, locking up as I rounded the front bumper. "Morning," I said, offering Tabitha a smile.

She returned it and gestured toward a small silver cage that sat at her feet. "Meet Tulip," she said.

Inside the cage a silvery-blue pixie hovered, her wings beating furiously. She was roughly the size of a softball and looked like a mix between a fairy and a small troll. Whereas fairies looked almost human, the pixie was a blend between human and creature, her eyes and ears disproportionately large. Her hands were also too big, with sharpened claws instead of fingertips.

A lustrous fairy dust followed her in a trail of gold that looked like glitter as she hovered and fluttered around in the cage, her dark, almost black eyes darting to and fro, never seeming to settle on something long enough to fully take it in.

"She looks excited," I said, looking up at Tabitha.

"She looks fun to chase," Selene said.

I frowned. "Don't even joke about that."

Selene rolled her eyes. "You have no sense of humor."

"Did you bring something that we can use to give her the scent of Lavender's magic? Or should we go inside?" Tabitha asked, casting a glance over her shoulder at Aunt Lavender's bungalow.

I quickly dug into my purse and pulled out Aunt Lavender's hairbrush. "Will this work? There's some of her hair in here."

"It should work just fine," Tabitha said, her tone dull.

I wasn't sure if her coffee just hadn't kicked in yet,

or if there was something more going on. I quickly pushed aside the thought, chalking it up to residual awkwardness.

"So, what do we do from here?" I asked. "It's been a long time since Aunt Lavender was taken from the house. She could be miles and miles from here, for all we know. Will her scent trail even be strong enough for this to work?"

Tabitha glanced at the cage. "Pixies like Tulip are well seasoned at this work. It's not just Lavender's scent she'll be able to pick up. It's deeper than that. It's more the scent of Lavender's unique magic signature. We all have one. It's like a fingerprint, unique to every witch."

I glanced at Selene. She gave a nod of confirmation.

Tabitha continued, "Tulip will leave a trail for us to follow. And whenever possible, she will do her best to stick to roads and trails, to make it easier for us to keep up, even doubling back when the trail goes off road."

"Wow." I peered down at the tiny being.

"I can't guarantee she'll be able to find Lavender's exact location, but she might be able to lead us to a new clue," Tabitha said. "It's going to take some patience though. She might lead us on a bit of a goose chase before she finds the strongest current of Lavender's magic."

"How many pixies are there like Tulip?"

Tabitha shook her head. "I'm not certain, but they are incredibly rare. The training process is intense, and most pixies don't have the attention span for the work. Pixies are also very selective when it comes to breeding, so it isn't easy to breed high-performing pixies together to up the chances of having a good bloodline, the way people do with purebred dogs."

"Got it." I nodded, though I was still a little overwhelmed by the information and stunned at our luck in securing the use of Tulip for the day. "Thanks again, Tabitha, for arranging this. It means a lot."

Tabitha hitched her satchel up a bit higher on her shoulder and gave me a curt nod. "It's not a problem. Now, are we ready to go? I thought we could take my car."

"Oh, of course. Sure." I headed for the passenger seat of Tabitha's rented SUV and found the door unlocked.

Only once Selene and I were buckled up did Tabitha pick up the small cage. She brought it around to the front of the car and opened the door. Tulip shot out like a hummingbird, flying high and fast, before zooming back down toward Tabitha.

"Here," Tabitha said, offering the hairbrush. "We need to find her."

Tulip scattered pixie dust over the hairbrush, then inhaled deeply, breathing in her own magic and Lavender's scent.

"I wish she had told us it was a magical scent, not an actual scent," I said to Selene. "I would have brought one of Aunt Lavender's magical instruments instead."

"If she needed something else, she would have said so," Selene replied. "Besides, I think it's best we don't let her inside Lavender's house."

"You still think she was here that night to try and steal something?"

Selene didn't get a chance to answer before Tabitha opened the driver's side door and hurried to get behind the wheel. "There she goes!" she exclaimed, looking excited for the first time.

Tulip took two laps around the perimeter of Lavender's house before she shot higher into the air and surged over the yard, and down the street, leading toward the center of town. As promised, she left a thick trail of golden dust in her wake, making it easy to follow her, even when we could no longer see her tiny body.

It took some time for the pixie to make her way through downtown Winterspell. She got hung up at all of Aunt Lavender's usual haunts: the fish market, the general store, the bookshop.

"This is getting ridiculous," Selene complained as we idled in front of the ice cream parlor, watching Tulip dive-bomb through the alleyway between it and the shop next door.

"Be patient, Selene. Tabitha said this might happen. Clearly these are all places where Aunt Lavender's scent trail and magic would be. We have to trust the process."

Tulip zoomed out of the alley and streaked off

down the sidewalk. Tabitha followed, not bothering to add her own take on the situation.

This time, Tulip headed out of town, toward the lake. My nerves cinched tighter with every passing mile as we left the downtown area behind and hit the highway leading into the more remote parts of Winter-spell. Aunt Lavender was an adventurer, but never in her own backyard. Whereas I loved nothing more than a weekend morning on the lake in my kayak, or hiking through the woods, Aunt Lavender reserved her outdoor adventures for her treasure hunts.

"This has to be something," I said, keeping my voice soft in an effort to rein in my growing excitement. "Aunt Lavender wouldn't be out here on her own. Right?" I asked Selene.

Selene sat at attention in my lap, her eyes focused on the view through the windshield. "No. Lavender wouldn't be out this far. Not by choice, at least."

Renewed determination set my jaw as I stared at the pixie's trail, almost forgetting to blink. Or breathe.

We reached a trailhead and Tulip paused, giving us time to catch up. Tabitha pulled her SUV over a patch of gravel that wasn't a designated parking spot but was off the road far enough to keep her vehicle from getting hit by other motorists.

Tulip waited for us to climb out of the vehicle and then she blitzed off up the trail.

"Let's go!" Selene exclaimed, already running for the trail.

I'd hiked the trail before, dozens of times. There weren't any buildings or outposts along the way. A new fear uncoiled in my belly as I followed Selene's lead. What if this was no longer a rescue mission? What if we were too late? The woods weren't a place to hide a kidnapping victim. But they were a place to dump a body.

I swallowed hard and tried to keep my dread in check.

Tabitha walked behind me, keeping her own thoughts to herself.

The sky was dismal and gray, with low-hanging, foggy cloud cover draping over us the farther up the hill we trekked. The exertion kept me warm, and after we'd gone a few miles, I stopped to peel off my coat, as my shirt clung to my back.

My stomach roiled with unease. We were hiking up into the mountainous terrain that surrounded the lake. I glanced to my left. The lake was off in the distance, placid and tranquil, majestic in the valley of the rolling hills that surrounded Winterspell like a protective, sturdy gate.

"Aunt Lavender, where are you?" I whispered to myself, staring out over the thick woods.

Tabitha moved ahead of me on the trail while I paused to catch my breath. After a few minutes, I began plodding along again, though my pace was slower than when we'd started. After another mile, maybe two, Tabitha was so far ahead I lost sight of her.

My short legs couldn't compete with her Amazonian physique.

I still had the golden trail of pixie dust to follow though, so I didn't worry about getting lost.

"Cora!" Selene cried from somewhere over a slope.

Grimacing, I broke into a shuffling jog, careful to keep my footing as I hurried up the hill. From the top, I could see Tabitha and Selene standing at the base of a steep rock-covered cliff. They were both staring straight up—at a shimmering swath of glittering pixie dust.

"What is it?" I asked, panting as I came to a stop beside them.

All I needed to do was look up to get the answer to my question. Tulip's trail led into the mouth of a cave carved into the side of the rocky cliff. It was a good twenty or thirty feet up, and while the cliffside wasn't one hundred perfect vertical, it was steep enough that we'd have a hard time climbing it without equipment.

"She thinks Lavender is in there?" Selene shook her head. "No way. The woman didn't go a day without complaining about her hip pain when she first got out of bed. She's in good shape for someone her age ... but this?"

"I agree," I said, still trying to catch my breath. "It doesn't make any sense. A kidnapper couldn't get her all the way here on their back. I mean unless our new theory is that Hercules himself is the assailant. And why bother bringing her here? Surely, there are other hiding places they could stash her."

I glanced at Tabitha. She crossed her arms, still peering up at the side of the cliff. "I don't know why, but that's where the trail leads."

Every red flag and alarm bell was ringing inside my head to turn around and make my way back down the mountain—but I couldn't bring myself to do it.

"Remember Mom's theory, about Aunt Lavender being somewhere her magic couldn't reach?" I said, looking to Selene. "What if there's something about the magic here, some property or some enchantment that's suppressing things?"

Selene cast a suspicious look around the woods. "Seems pretty normal to me. But—"

My heart jumped. "But what?"

"Lavender might not be here now, but maybe she was here, at one point in time," Selene replied, her words slow. "We've been finding all sorts of her secret little hidey-holes over the past few weeks. What if she has something hidden up there in that cave? Something that's been there for years, decades even."

I peered up the steep cliffside again. Tulip's trail twinkled in a ray of sunlight breaking through the evergreens. "You think so?"

Beside me, Tabitha began to fidget. She shifted her weight and scratched her fingernails at the base of her neck.

"Do you have to pee or something?" Selene asked her.

"No…" Tabitha trailed off. "But maybe you're right. This is probably a mistake. We should just go back to town."

"Go back?" I asked. "Why?"

"Tulip probably made a mistake. Maybe the wind carried the scent here, or something." She picked at her nails, not making eye contact with me.

My eyes narrowed at Tabitha. "You said she was highly trained. This can't just be a mistake. Something is up there."

I shook my head and lifted my foot onto the first rock protruding from the wall. "I'm not going back now." I grasped the next rock, testing to see if it was wide enough. "We've come too far to turn around."

"Cora," Selene said, a dark warning in her tone.

"I'm fine, Selene," I snapped. "I have my magic to break my fall if that should happen. Just be quiet and let me concentrate."

"Please!" Tabitha shouted. "Don't do this, Cora! It's not worth it."

Ignoring them, I climbed to the next foothold. I'd gone to those rock-climbing gyms before. I knew the basics. And should I slip, I thought I would have enough time to cast a bit of air magic to soften my landing.

Selene growled something at Tabitha, but my thoughts were too loud, and I missed her exact words.

"Cora, Selene is right," Tabitha called up to me. "Please come down. We'll find another way."

Gritting my teeth, I reached for my next handhold. The rock gave way, and I slipped. "I just need to—" I grunted and paused, "keep—my—footing. Careful steps—"

"Cora, stop!"

Tabitha's barking voice startled me as I tried another rock. The toe of my boot slipped on some loose debris and my stomach bottomed out as I gripped the side of the cliff with my fingertips.

Sweat rolled down my forehead. I couldn't risk taking one hand off the rock wall long enough to wipe it away. It wasn't like me to be so unprepared. But then, I hadn't expected to go free climbing.

"She—she's not in there." Tabitha's voice crumpled. Her bossy, commanding tone was gone.

I went still, not moving a muscle. "What?"

"She's not in that cave, Cora," Tabitha repeated. "This was all just a—"

"Just a *what*?" Selene exclaimed. I couldn't risk twisting around to look at my familiar, but from the sound of her voice, I imagined she'd launched herself onto Tabitha's chest and embedded her claws in the front of her expensive leather jacket.

"It was a lie," Tabitha said on a heavy exhale. "All of it."

Something broke inside my chest. Surprise. Bewilderment ... pain. It all coiled together in a thick, heavy braid that pulled tight and snapped.

"I'm so sorry, Cora," Tabitha continued with a sob. "Please come down so I can explain."

"What is there to explain?" Selene growled. "You lied to us! For what? Why lead us on and bring us all this way out here? For laughs? What are you, some kind of sick puppy? You get your jollies watching other people suffer? We ought to throw your bony butt right off this cliff!"

"Selene!" I ground my teeth and shifted my focus. Instead of up to the destination, I needed to find a way back down to the trail. Stars, this would be so much easier if I had a rope.

"I swear, Cora. If you don't let me handle this—"

"You're my familiar. If you kill her, I'll be the one they march off to prison," I said, sliding my hand back to its previous spot on the wall. All I needed to do was retrace my steps.

"Only if they find the body!" Selene growled.

I pinched my eyes closed for a moment and drew in a breath. "Selene, please. Just help me get back down, okay?"

"And then I can claw her eyes out?"

"I'll let ya know," I grunted.

I made it to the last step and took a tiny leap. Once I was on solid ground, my knees wobbled, but I quickly found my footing. As soon as I did, I marched up to Tabitha. "Tell us what's going on, right now," I demanded, my voice so deep and low it sounded foreign to me, as if the words had come from someone else's mouth.

Beside me, Selene was vibrating, like a buzz saw ready to slice through anything that got in her way.

Tabitha's face was paler than usual as her gaze flickered from me to the cave and back again. "All that's waiting in the cave is a sweater I stole from Lavender's house the night you guys found me sneaking around."

"Why would you do that?" I stared at her, dumbfounded, grasping at straws to make sense of it all.

Tabitha looked down at the rocks under her boots. Her features contorted with guilt. "I was hired to keep you and Selene distracted," she confessed, not even having the decency to look me in the eye as she spilled the awful truth.

"So, it was all for nothing? You were just here to keep us running around in circles like a bunch of fools?" Selene asked.

Tabitha lifted her face and blinked at us, her eyes bleak. "Yes."

"I should have your head on a spike, you know," Selene began.

"Everybody just calm down," I said, standing between the two to keep Selene from digging her claws into Tabitha's eyeballs.

I raised my hands and looked at Selene. "I'm just as livid as you, but we need to figure this out—"

Tabitha shrieked.

Selene's eyes grew wide with horror. "What in the hot fudge sundae is happening to her?"

I spun around and looked at Tabitha. Her eyes were wide with shock. Her body was rigid. Her arms were stiff at her sides, her feet rooted to the ground. Inch by inch, a stony gray substance began trailing its way up Tabitha's body, starting at her ankles, then to her knees, crawling up her thighs, her torso.

"I can't move!" she yelled. Her eyes went wild with panic. "Help me!"

"Selene!" I exclaimed, my own body frozen with panic. "What's happening? What do we do?"

Selene hijacked some of my magic and sent an unknown spell at Tabitha's chest. Pink sparks bounced off the rough gray substance, like a bouncy ball hitting tile flooring.

Tabitha began to gurgle and choke. She gasped for air, but it came out more like a cough. Her eyes glazed over as her face began to turn gray too, stiffening and causing her skin to become rough and rigid.

She opened her mouth. "Stay away from—" she warned, but her voice became strangled, and she couldn't manage to get the rest out before her entire face seized.

The spell sealed itself with an ominous *crack*, and there before us stood famed adventurer, Tabitha Hardwick, formed entirely out of stone.

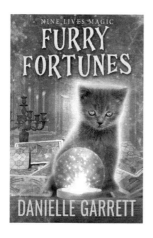

AFTER A STUNNING BETRAYAL knocks me for a loop, I don't know who I can trust. The trail to finding Aunt Lavender is warmer than ever—but also more dangerous.

Can a visit to the local psychic provide the final clue? Or will her inclinations land us in the crosshairs of the kidnapper?

There's only one way to find out, and all I can hope is the crystal ball is clear enough to light the way.

Get your copy of Furry Fortunes and return to Winterspell today!

Sign up for my newsletter here: www. DanielleGarrettBooks.com/newsletter

Join the Bat Wings Book Club here: www.facebook. com/groups/daniellegarrettreadergroup

. . .

THANK YOU FOR READING. I hope you enjoyed your visit to Winterspell.

Danielle Garrett

www.DanielleGarrettBooks.com

In Winterspell Lake there are things darker than midnight...

Sprinkles and Sea Serpents is the first book in a brand new paranormal cozy mystery series by Danielle Garrett. This series features magic, mystery, family squabbles, sassy heroines, and a mysterious monster hunter—all with a little sugar sprinkled on top.

Find the Sugar Shack Witch Mysteries on Amazon.

ALSO BY DANIELLE GARRETT

One town. Two spunky leading ladies.
More magic than you can shake a wand at.
Welcome to Beechwood Harbor.

Come join the fun in Beechwood Harbor, the little town where witches, shifters, ghosts, and vamps all live, work, play, and—mostly—get along!

The two main series set in this world are the Beechwood Harbor Magic Mysteries and the Beechwood Harbor Ghost Mysteries.

In the following pages you will find more information about those books, as well as my other works available.

Alternatively, you can find a complete reading list on my website:

www.DanielleGarrettBooks.com

ABOUT THE AUTHOR

Danielle Garrett has been an avid bookworm for as long as she can remember, immersing herself in the magic of far-off places and the rich lives of witches, wizards, princesses, elves, and some wonderful everyday heroes as well. Her love of reading naturally blossomed into a passion for storytelling, and today, she's living the dream she's nurtured since the second grade—crafting her own worlds and characters as an author.

A proud Oregonian, Danielle loves to travel but always finds her way back to the Pacific Northwest, where she shares her life with her husband and their beloved menagerie of animal companions.

Visit Danielle today at her website or say "hello" on Facebook.

www.DanielleGarrettBooks.com